The

CRIPPLED

LADY OF PERIBONKA

By

JAMES OLIVER CURWOOD

Illustrations by

JOHN ALAN MAXWELL

Fredonia Books
Amsterdam, The Netherlands

The Crippled Lady of Peribonka

by
James Oliver Curwood

ISBN: 1-4101-0758-2

Copyright © 2004 by Fredonia Books

Reprinted from the 1929 edition

Fredonia Books
Amsterdam, The Netherlands
http://www.fredoniabooks.com

In order to make original editions of historical works available to scholars at an economical price, this facsimile of the original edition of 1929 is reproduced from the best available copy and has been digitally enhanced to improve legibility, but the text remains unaltered to retain historical authenticity.

THE CRIPPLED LADY OF PERIBONKA

Chapter 1

THIS story is going to start like a lesson in geography. This is because it is largely a chronicle of real events in human lives. History, whether of things or people, rests upon the basic necessity of possessing certain aspects of situation which we encompass within the terms of latitude and longitude. The following narrative would quite profoundly miss its real drama if it were to ignore the points of the compass and the manner in which Fate played with them to bring about an unusual combination of ends.

We will begin with Peribonka. Peribonka is a quaint little French-Canadian village which nestles on the shore of the glorious Peribonka River, four miles above Lac St. Jean, in the Province of Quebec. It is made up almost entirely of a single row of thirty

3

or forty houses, all of which face the river. Should one adventure a little farther into the wilderness after having made the wonderful Saguenay trip up from Quebec to Ha Ha Bay or Chicoutimi and come to know Peribonka for himself, he will understand why the houses are situated with no neighbors or obstructions between them and the river. For the river is a living, breathing, God-sent thing to the French-speaking people of the place, about whose drowsy lives there still remains, like a sweet-scented veil of old lavender lace, the picturesque simplicity of their great-great-grandfathers of a hundred and fifty years ago. Though it is situated at the very edge of the Northern wilderness, Peribonka is so old that the ghosts of some of Roberval's men haunt it, and Roberval came up the Saguenay in the days of Cartier.

In contrast to the roaring, passionate Mistassini, fifteen miles away, the Peribonka is peculiarly like the men and women and

4

children who inhabit a few acres of its shores. It has, I believe, given to them much of their character, for of all the people in the habitant country those of Peribonka are the gentlest and most lovable. It is a third of a mile wide, clear and sweet, but quite shallow, with white sandbars that are ceaselessly changing and shifting, and which are alive with birds from spring until autumn. It reaches hundreds of miles into the mysterious and largely unmapped timberlands of the farther North, into the edge of which the ax of the pulpwood cutter has just begun to go. Even in the floodtimes of spring it is not an angry or menacing river, and in winter it is so genially smooth and well frozen that the habitant farmers use it for their horse-and-cutter races, or as a trail by which to come to town. In spite of its great size and the vast forces behind it, the kindness and gentleness of its nature must have made its people what they are. The men are truthful, their morals are right, they believe in God as well as in spirits, they are clean and courteous and hospitable. The women are bright eyed, clear skinned, unrouged, unbobbed, pretty. The children are allowed to smoke pipes from the age of seven or eight, but this ancient sin of the habitant is overshadowed by many fine and beautiful qualities. These people are always looking toward the river, in the evening when they go to bed, in the morning when they get up. They have built their picturesque little church facing it, and the good Father sleeps with his bedroom window opening upon it. The local cemetery occupies an acre of hallowed ground within a hundred feet of the water's edge. A venerable monastery is built at the mouth of it. Even the man stirring his vat of curd in the community cheese factory can look from his task upon its restful, smoothly flowing surface, dotted with snowy breasts of shifting sands and gay with the flashing wings of innumerable birds.

Back from the cheer of the river and encircling the town is the country—a narrow rim of habitant farms first, some that are old and others with the stumps lying about them freshly pulled, and beyond these are the unending miles of a wilderness that is hard and rough, and which still invites the fiercest contests with man after a hundred and fifty years of his presence—a land with huge reaches of "burns," in which there are blueberries enough to feed the world, a country filled with dangers and hardships, and which, unlike the river, resents the progress of human forces and retreats slowly and grudgingly before it.

Until quite recently the two happiest people in the village of Peribonka were Maria Chapdelaine and her husband Samuel, of whom Louis Hemon wrote. They are still happy, although Samuel is a bit overcast at present because of a financial loss which has come to him. For years Samuel has run his little store and Maria her kitchen, in which she prepares delectable meals for the few transients who come their way, and until this recent time to which I have referred, there is good reason to believe she was the happiest woman in her little world.

Now there is another. They call her the Crippled Lady. She is often seen sitting on the wide veranda of a quaint little home in a garden of flowers just this side of the church. There is a road which completely encircles Lac St. Jean, connecting the villages and farms in its narrow rim of civilization, and during the tourist season occasional automobiles pass through Peribonka. Their occupants always stare at the Crippled Lady if she happens to be on her porch. She is a vision of loveliness which one cannot easily forget. Women talk about her, and men silently bear away a picture of her in their hearts. Her beauty, if one has only a moment's contemplation of it, strikes almost with a shock. It is Slavic—thick, dark, shining hair drawn smoothly back, a face clearly white as a nun's, unforgettable eyes, a slim, beautiful figure

8

in a big chair—*and something else.* It is that other thing which photographs her so vividly and so permanently upon one's consciousness. Perhaps it is some time before one realizes that what he has seen is not beauty alone but *happiness.* Above all other things, that it what makes the Crippled Lady beautiful. It seems to clothe her in a kind of phosphorescent glow of loveliness that is ethereal. One sees it in her hair as well as in her eyes, and after one has heard her voice there is no longer any mystery about it. The Crippled Lady, who cannot walk, who cannot stand alone, is happy, and she covets nothing which God has not already given her. Her voice tells you that.

The people of Peribonka love this charming foreigner, who has made her home among them. The women are not jealous of her. She makes the significance of purity and beauty nearer and more comprehensive for the men. The Church prayed for her when she was very sick. She is of all religions, just

9

loving God, so that even the sternest of the monks in their grim white walls down near the lake speak and think of her tenderly. The children worship her, and the big, wide porch of her home has become a shrine for them. In Peribonka youth still continues to grow up into manhood and womanhood believing with great faith in the visible existence of spirits, both good and bad, and in the varied and frequent manifestations of a Divine interest and watchfulness. So the children have come to believe that it was a miracle which sent the Crippled Lady through the doors of death and then brought her safely back again, that she might remain with them always. Even the mothers and fathers believe this, just as surely as they believe it is a sin to steal from one's neighbor or speak falsehood against him. "Thus works the hand of God," the good Father has said. So the Church believes it, too.

They all know her story. And that story is an epic which will live for a long time in the country about Lac St. Jean. I doubt if it will die until the so-called progress of industrially active man thrusts up its grimy hand and inundates it, along with the quaintness and beauty and satisfying nearness to God of living up there.

It is this story I have set out to tell, with a bit of geography to begin with.—who the Crippled Lady is and why she is there, how she bravely tried to give up her life for another woman's husband, and why she lives to-day so happily in Peribonka.

Chapter II

IT IS unusual that an Indian should be born in one of the wealthiest families in New York.

Yet it happened.

A traveler to the city of Brantford, Ontario, will find within a few miles of the town a little church built for the Indians by King George the Third, and close about it an old cemetery, in which rests the dust of the last of the great Iroquois warriors and chiefs. In a tomb built of stone, which is green with age and moss, lies Thayendanegea, greatest of all the Mohawks, and more commonly known as Joseph Brant. Readers of the romance, as well as the fact of history, may recall the day when Sir William Johnson, the King's right arm in the Colonies, first saw Thayendanegea's sister. He was attending a muster of his county militia when an officer came galloping by with a beautiful Indian girl of sixteen riding laughingly behind him. Sir William, whose wife had recently died, caught a vision of lovely dark eyes and of flowing black hair streaming in a cloud behind a form of rare symmetry and grace, and in that moment the heart of the lonely and susceptible widower was smitten so deeply that evening found Molly Brant in Johnson Castle, where she remained, thenceforth its mistress and the idol of its proprietor.

Geography and history skip a hundred and thirty-five years after this event until they arrive at the birth of the Indian boy on Fifth Avenue.

When James Kirke married Molly Craddock neither thought very much about the strain of Indian blood in Molly's veins, except that Molly was always secretly proud of it. Kirke was not the kind of man to boast of ancestors, or even to think about them, for

After a hundred and thirty-five years the blood of the lovely Molly Brant had come into its own.

he had one consuming ambition from the beginning, and that was to pyramid his inherited millions into ever-increasing financial power. He became so completely absorbed in this task that after a few years Molly was left very largely to whatever dreams she may have had of the picturesque and romantic past, and to an absorbing love for her young son, Paul. She told him many of the pretty stories and some of the tragic ones which deeds had written in the lives of their ancestors, and twice she went with him to the ancient burial-place near Brantford and sat beside the tomb of Thayendanegea, and tried to make him see as clearly as herself the stirring days when Molly Brant came with tresses flying before Sir William Johnson.

From the hour Paul opened his eyes to the light of life he had in him the soul of an Indian. After a hundred and thirty-five years the blood of the lovely Molly Brant had come into its own. One would not have guessed it from the boy's physical appearance, for he was light rather than dark, with blue eyes and blond hair. But the modern Molly, who lived in a palace, with a Crœsus for a husband, saw what was happening as the years passed by. Her boy grew lean of face and figure. His cheek bones were a little high. His love for the outdoors became a passion. He was quieter than other boys, and about him was an aloofness which his father did not notice particularly, but which she measured with accurate knowledge. She made it possible for him to spend his vacations in the woods, and each time he returned she knew that something had been taken away from him and a little more of the other thing put in its place. She tried to interest him in the achievements of his father, but he was more deeply concerned in the proper way for a woodsman to chop down a tree. The servants thought he was queer, and loved his quiet and stoical kindness, which was many years older than his age. Most boys would have lived up to the princely grandeur of his environment.

20

To Paul it meant less than a tree with birds singing in its branches.

In his thirteenth year came three events of vital importance in the shaping of his future. First his mother died. No one would ever know the terrible, unhealing wound it cut in Paul's heart. It was James Kirke, the hardened and power-seeking juggernaut of flesh and blood who went to pieces when he discovered that death had been fearless enough to cross his path. One would have thought he had been a lover to the woman who was dead. His agony was like a storm, tragic for a time, and quickly over. He settled back into the fierce strife of his money-getting by the time Paul began to grieve. But the shadow and the fact of death changed him a little. He saw himself alone, except for his son. And this son, after years of passing interest on his part, became the kernel of his plans and ambitions. He was now king. Some day his boy would be king. And it was his desire and his decision that he should be a greater king than himself. Pride fired his resolution.

But here the geographical genius of Fate again stepped in with humors of its own. In another Fifth Avenue home a baby girl was born to the wife of Kirke's most implacable financial enemy, Henry Durand. A few months later, three thousand miles or more away, an immigrant ship left for America. On board this ship was a clear-eyed, hopeful woodcutter from the mountain country of Central Europe. With him were his wife and baby. They were an important three. The sea might have swallowed them and no one would have cared very much, for their adventure was only one of millions of a similar kind. The immigrant baby's fortune began and ended with the few little clothes she wore. The other baby was worth millions one second after she came into the world. The immigrant baby came in under the Statue of Liberty on the day Paul was sent away to school.

Paul continued to grow up, and with equal steadiness his father continued to amass fortune and influence. By this time James Kirke would not have accepted the presidency of the United States. It was his passion to smash and break down, then devour and build up—until someone called him the Anaconda, a name which fitted him so well that the newspapers would have used it had they dared. Kirke was always within the legal boundaries of his country's laws. He absorbed shipping companies, railroads, coal mines, and timberlands, and sent out his engineers to corner vast water-power rights. From an industrial point of view he was constructively an asset, for wherever he broke down or consumed small activities he built up larger ones. But morally and ethically his brain was inspired by a covetous and avid desire to rule. He was intolerant of rivalry, and this brought him each year in closer and more deadly contact with the equally far-reaching interests of Henry Durand. The titanic struggle between these two Goliaths of financial and industrial activities is a part of Wall Street history. The more interesting sory of Paul and the two babies is known only to a few, chiefly about Lac St. Jean.

That his father married again soon after Molly Kirke's death and had another son did not hurt Paul, except that it made him grieve more deeply for his mother and added to his loneliness. He got along only fairly well in college, because he could never completely shackle his mind to duties that were confined within stone and brick walls. It took him an extra year to finish an engineering course, and after that he was never happy except when in the open spaces. In a business way he was interested only in his father's timberlands and such water-power projects as were situated in the wilderness. As a whole he was a disappointment to his parent.

One restless night the greatest of all his ideas came to James Kirke. The next day he

24

went boldly and in friendly spirit to the office of Henry Durand, and for hours the two colossi talked over Kirke's suggestion that their interests be combined into one giant force of countless millions. They parted friends. In a little while they were seen at the clubs together. Later the all-powerful Kirke-Durand Corporation became a reality. The flinty old warriors worked hand in hand, their assets multiplied. Their palatial homes were scenes of mutual intercourse. Their wives were intimate. Their children became acquainted.

In his thirty-second year Paul married Claire Durand.

In his thirty-eighth year, the son of one of the richest men in New York, he was officially in charge of the huge engineering work on the Mistassini River in the wilderness north of Lac St. Jean and had been three years on the job.

During these three years he had known Carla Haldan.

He was thinking of Carla as he looked from a window of his bungalow office on the hill down over the vast and naked workings of an engineering achievement which was costing fifty million dollars. He felt no exultation or thrill of pride, and in his eyes was a far-back, somber gloom. What he saw was to him an unending and nauseous pit into which a steady and monotonous drizzle of rain was falling. Everywhere was smoke and steel and distant roar and miles of sticky, slimy clay. There were fifteen hundred men on the job below him working in three eight-hour shifts, and neither darkness nor storm could stop them. Six hundred of the human machines were working now in the wet and mud, and he could see them moving and crawling about like ants at their labor. In his mind they added nothing to the scene, unless it was to give grimmer reality to a hell that was smoking and boiling over. All about them locomotives were running up and down with their lines of cars, clamshells as big as houses

From his chair he could look to an unbroken sweep of country.

were smashing their hungry mouths into the obstinate clay, engines and tackle were grinding and roaring, derricks were creaking under weights of steel, stone crushers were breaking up train loads of rock, cement mixers were spewing out streams of engineering lava—everywhere a rumble and din, everywhere the fierce and heartbreaking labor of men, everywhere the ugliness and madness of a man-made place of torment.

Paul was thinking this even with Carla Haldan in his mind. He could see the gray-white sluices and dykes with their cement and steel walls, and the monster sections of the almost completed dam, which was to harness Northern waters to the production of light and power for twenty million people. He could see the structural skeletons of giant power houses which were to flash their mighty forces over the land. Three years of human effort and millions in capital lay under his eyes. Yet about it all was only one excusable and beautiful thing for him. That

29

was the rim of wilderness, the green and black and purple boundaries of the forest which clung like a frame about the workings, with its billowing seas of spruce and balsam and pine reaching far back into the rain-filled skies beyond.

His contemplation of the scene in the valley was interrupted by a voice at his office door, and he turned to greet the most intimate of his friends in the field, Colin Derwent, who was the company's medical man. Even on rainy days, and with his boots clogged with mud, Derwent was a cheerful soul. With his Frenchy little moustache, his smooth cheeks, his liveliness of movement, and his appreciation of all phases of life, he continued to bear the appearance of a boy, though he had filled an important chair in medicine in Johns Hopkins.

He nodded to Paul, dropped off his rubber coat, and began to fill his pipe as he looked out over the workings.

"I wish all the boys in the world could

30

stand at this window and see what's going on down there," he said. "That idea gets into my head every time I come here. It would fill 'em with ambition, show 'em what can be done, give 'em something to live and work for. Rotten day, isn't it?"

"Rotten," agreed Paul.

"But for a man who's done *that*—it ought to be sunshine all the time," added Derwent, lighting his pipe and puffing at it with great contentment. "Splendid work, Paul. Something to be proud of all your life. Something——"

"I hate it," interrupted Paul. "I've hated it from the beginning. I've hated it for three years."

Derwent nodded. "I know it."

Paul turned from the window with a fiercely eloquent gesture. At thirty-eight his lean, lithe figure was more like an Indian's than when he was a boy. There was something in the cut of his chin, his neck, his shoulders, and the look in his eyes which

31

seemed to set him widely apart from the scene he had moodily surveyed a moment before. His features were so steadily immobile they might have been molded out of the steel down in the pit. Shadows were hidden behind them, restless and troubled shadows, which revealed themselves only now and then like ghosts whose grief could not always be kept behind walls of flesh. His eyes were a deeper blue than when his mother had known him, and they held a chained something which was forever struggling against the powerful will of the man. Occasionally the prisoner was released, and when this happened there was a singular, far-seeing, almost poetic beauty in them, and the steel went out of his flesh, so that he seemed all at once to come under the passing warmth of an influence other than that which had become so deeply rooted in his life.

Derwent's analytical mind had arrived at the truth of the matter a long time ago. He nodded again and repeated: "I know you

32

don't like it. But it's a great work just the same."

Paul looked at him with a grim smile, and Derwent surrounded himself with a cloud of smoke.

"Do you think I am quite a fool, Colin? Do you really believe I could be on a job of this kind for three years without getting a pretty accurate measurement of myself? The fraud of it all makes me sick! The flattery of my friends—everybody treating me as if I were an omnisciently powerful godhead of some kind! I tell you it's all a lie, and I hate it. I'm glad I didn't build that outrage down there. I'm glad there isn't a mark of my hand upon it. Good God! I would die by inches rather than destroy a beautiful river for a thing like that—desecrate a masterpiece for a few dollars' profit, prostitute a gift which God put there when the world was made, that a few worms like you and me may turn it to our selfish ends. If there is a Power that mounts the storm and walks upon the wind it ought to strike us dead for transforming a paradise into *that!*"

He walked to the window and pointed down. Never had Derwent or any other man seen such strange passion in Paul's face. Weeks and months and years of gnawing torment had at last broken through the dam he had built up about his emotions, and he spoke words which yesterday he would have throttled in his breast.

"Fifty million dollars in and about that hole before it is finished, Derwent," he said. "My father's money. That is why I am here. A score of engineers are on this job, and every one of them is better fitted to fill my place than I. There are men about me whose minds and brains make mine a child's in comparison. *They* have done the work, not I. Respectfully they submit suggestions when they know they should be commands. Yet they are slaves to my whims and desires as long as they remain on this work. I am the strutting figurehead of a financial monarchy. I hate

34

that pit down there. I hate the millions going into it. I take no pride in what seems to thrill you all. If I filled my proper place I would be among the men digging and messing myself with clay, earning my six dollars a day. But I'm here instead. I do not have to succeed simply because I cannot fail. My father's millions attend to that. The millions cannot lose. They are all-powerful next to the Lord Jehovah. They get you and hold you, and you cannot break away. My father has never got away from them for a day's play in his life. And they've got me. I hate them, but that doesn't help. No matter where I go they follow me, haunt me, tie me hand and foot, grimace at me, and mock me. They leave me nothing to fight for, unless it is to destroy them. Sometimes I have had that terrible thought. I would like to see those millions shrivel up and die. I would like to feel the necessities of life with my naked hands. I would like to feel the joy of knowing that I had to work or go hungry. What a thrill that must give one!"

He turned toward Derwent again, trying to stem the tide of his emotion with a smile.

"Pardon me. It's a gloomy day and I feel like raving. But I did love that glorious river before we cut it into ribbons. If my father would head his millions the other way and save such things instead of destroying them, I'd be quite happy. As it is, I suppose I must carry on until the damned thing's finished."

"You owe yourself an apology," Derwent remonstrated, pocketing his pipe. "The engineers and your father's money are making the job a success, of course. But do you ever think of morale? That's a big thing, a mighty big thing. And it is what you have kept alive in the camps up and down the river for the last three years. You're too serious, you don't laugh enough, you don't join much in our parties and excitements, *but people like you*. That is what pulls the trick. Even the old heads, the engineers who worked in Egypt and Panama, love to be with you. There isn't a jealous man in the workings. To have made that condition possible is an achievement which makes you the most valuable human asset in the organization."

"It is good of you to say that," acknowledged Paul. "Funny why I should feel so strangely out of humor to-day. I think Carla's mother is getting on my nerves. Have you seen her recently?"

"This morning."

"And you still insist there is no hope?"

"Positively. I had Dr. Thiedmere come up from Quebec, as you requested. He gives her even less time than I. Dr. Rollins agrees with him. It can't be more than three or four months, I think. Mrs. Haldan knows she is going to die and talks to us very calmly about it. She isn't afraid. The thought of it doesn't seem to cast a shadow over her motherly sweetness. She is keeping herself that way for Carla's sake. If it were not for Carla the thing wouldn't be such a tragedy."

"I know. It's Carla," said Paul. "Sudden sickness and death, like my own mother's, isn't so terrible. But seeing it coming, waiting for it, counting the days and weeks—must be horrible. Carla is losing everything she has when her mother goes. I'm wondering what she will do."

"Go on working among the children. She told my wife that yesterday. When the company's school closes here she will find another. I cannot understand her—quite. She is lovelier than Hebe, and so lovable that half the men I know worship her. Yet she favors one no more than another. She is twenty-five, Lucy-Belle says. They like each other and have had their confidences. Lucy-Belle is a clever little witch at getting to the bottom of things, and she says there is a love affair in Carla's life, a broken one, which makes it impossible for Carla to love any other man or marry. Carla told her that."

Paul looked out of the window again, with his back to Derwent.

"What a rotter I am to blow up as I did a few minutes ago," he exclaimed. "But I was thinking of Carla and the damnable obstinacy of life. Mine has been one way, Carla's another. I was born rich; she came over an immigrant baby. I did nothing but grow up; she fought with the pertinacity of her race for an education after her father died, got it, and has been fighting for her own and her mother's existence ever since. I'm a man. She's a woman. I stand here and sympathize with myself and curse my luck for being what I am while she bears up like a soldier under her burdens. I saw her this morning. It was wet, soggy, gloomy, but she smiled. The sadness of all the world is back of that smile, but it doesn't spoil its sweetness or its cheer. She makes me feel how small I am and how inconsequential all this work is down in the pit. I always fit her in with things somewhere else—in the mountains, in the forests, in places where a lot of people are not about. I would give all this down here

—if it were mine to give—could I save her mother for her!"

Derwent put on his raincoat.

"We all feel that way about it. And—we're helpless. Lucy-Belle wants you to come over to supper. Will you?"

"Thanks. Tell Lucy-Belle she is an angel to think of me so often. I'll come."

Chapter III

PAUL sat at his desk after Derwent had gone. From his chair he could look through another window to a clean and unbroken sweep of country where the forest had stood, and where now were rows of cottages built for the men whose wives and families had come with them to the workings. He could see Lucy-Belle Derwent's home, and not far from it the cottage in which Carla Haldan and her mother lived. He had often felt an emptiness of heart and a great longing when his eyes rested upon these half hundred homes of the women whose love and loyalty had urged them to follow their husbands' fortunes. His wife was not among them. Only twice in three years had she come up to what she had called "these horrible woods," and then she had departed after a day or

43

two. Her picture was on his desk. He knew she was beautiful, in a vivid, golden way. But her beauty had never touched him deeply. It had been for him like a beauty of a flower made by a master craftsman from paper or glass, without the rare, sweet perfume which should have been a part of it, and for which he had yearned all his life. He had thought of her as a lovely bird in a gilded cage—and the cage was the palace which he called his home. It was a senseless thought, for the cage did not hold her often. She was in Europe now. Last year it was Egypt. Next year it would be some other far-away place.

Behind Paul's dispassionate features was another being of poetry, of dreams, of hoped-for things—all crushed back and held behind the steely obligations of his life. He had been true to the woman on his desk, just as he knew she was true to him, and whatever he had wanted in woman he tried to build up about her. He wanted to love her. He did love the ideal which he created of her, a kind of

44

dream woman, whom he endowed with a great love for himself and placed in one of the cottages which he could see from his office window.

He did not realize that during recent months he had clothed this ideal a little at a time in what he found in Carla Haldan.

Yesterday he had received a letter from Paris. It was friendly and full of interest, with here and there the delicate little play of words which Claire was fond of employing—quite a long letter, too, but without a line in it to say she wanted him or was looking forward to the time when she would see him again. She must have written it in her dressing room, with her hair down, for one of the long, fine-spun golden filaments had got into the letter somehow, and at first he wanted to believe she had put it there. Then he recalled that previous to this letter it had been five weeks since she had communicated with him. So there was no sentiment about it. Just accident. With Carla it was different.

Flowers which she cut from her garden were always on his desk. A vase of gorgeous autumn nasturtiums was there now. Usually Carla sent them over by one of her school children, but occasionally she brought them herself. She made no display of the act, nor was there a motive in it, except the one inspired by kindness. Paul knew she would have done the same thing if his wife had been there. The two had met. Claire, who was half an artist, had gone into a little ecstasy of delight over Carla's quiet and unforgettable type of beauty. After their visit in Paul's office, made interesting because Claire had been in the country where the other was born, Carla had seemed to bear in her heart a warm and tender feeling for the woman to whose husband she brought flowers. A curious fact had come out between them. They were the same age—twenty-five—both born on the same day. Funny, Paul had thought, how much two women could learn from each other in a short time.

46

*One of the long, fine-spun filaments had got into
the letter . . .*

Paul was looking at the Haldan cottage as he sat thinking, and saw Carla come out into the rain and turn down the cinder path toward his office. In a little while he knew she was on her way to visit him. He stood up to watch the slim figure in its close-fitting silken raincoat and hood. There was something about Carla which was always goddess-like, even in drizzle and mud. Yet she was not really tall, as he measured women. He had observed that her head came just a little above his shoulder. Her slimness gave her the appearance of greater height than she possessed.

These things Paul had begun to notice. He could not tell the color of Lucy-Belle's eyes, but he knew that Carla's were a clear and beautiful gray, and that the dark lashes which covered them were very long and fine. He observed only casually Lucy-Belle's hair, but Carla's, he knew, was always closely coiled and drawn back so softly and silkily smooth from her forehead that more than once he had felt the desire to put his hand upon it. He knew how she would come in through his door, hiding her grief as much as she could from the world, that its gloom might not oppress or embarrass others. To have a mother at home, dying, and then to smile, was—Carla.

He met her at the door, and Carla had wet, fresh nasturtiums in her hand. The drift of the rain had been in her face, and little diamonds of water were clinging to her lashes and pale cheeks. A glow of greeting was in her eyes and the smile was on her lips, as he knew they would be. He helped her off with her coat and hood, and her dark hair was just as he had expected it. More than ever, on this particular afternoon, the desire to touch it came over him.

She had objected a little to taking off her raincoat.

"I want to talk with you for only a few moments, if the inconvenience isn't too great," she said.

50

"And I want to talk with you—for a long time," he replied. "I am not working, not even dictating, and I have let my secretary go. I have felt peculiarly the desire to do nothing this afternoon. The day has been empty and blue, and it brightened only when I saw you coming down the path. I have been thinking about you—quite a bit."

He had never said as much as this, with the steely shutters let down from his eyes so that the other man within him was looking through. A flush so faint that Paul did not notice it gathered in Carla's cheeks.

"Thinking of me?" she inquired. "That is kind of you. I like to be thought about— pleasantly. And you could not think otherwise of me when I bring you flowers."

He was glad she had spoken about her flowers.

"They have been an encouragement and an inspiration to me for a long time," he said. "No matter how annoying my work or how gloomy the day, they are always like

51

a cheering friend smiling at me from my desk. They have helped to make a philosopher of me, and have strengthened my conviction that the little thoughtful things we do for one another, and not the big ones, are what make life worth living. No amount of money could create the kindness which is in your heart when you bring me flowers. Therefore the act, and the sentiment which comes with it, are priceless."

The warmth in her cheeks deepened into a delicate rose flush of color.

"I am glad my flowers have seemed friendly to you. They are always that to me. I love them just as I love trees. If it were not that their crowning mission is to bring us comfort and solace, I should hate to pick them. Sometimes it seems to me like killing beautiful things with souls in them. I feel the same way when I see a tree cut down."

Her gaze rested upon the picture of his wife.

"I often think of Mrs. Kirke when I pick

my nasturtiums," she added. "She is of their
beauty, colorful, vivid, full of gold and life.
Is she well?"

"I believe so. She is in Paris. I received a
letter from her yesterday in which she speaks
of you. She says she has not forgotten her
threat to come up and paint you some day.
That will be exciting, her third visit in three
years."

She caught the inflection of irony in his
voice, though he was not trying to reveal it.
The knowledge of his loneliness sometimes
oppressed her. It was one reason why she
picked flowers for him. And she was always
saying something nice for the woman whose
picture was on his desk and whose life was
so apart from his, so infinitely separated
from everything in which he might have
found happiness.

"I have tried to grow hyacinths about my
cottage," she said. "But they won't live. They
die. I love them and have given them every
care, and I make myself believe they would

like to grow for me if they could. I told Mrs. Kirke of my experience when she was here a year ago, and you should have seen her eyes light up. 'I am like that,' she said. 'I would die if I had to live up here. Paul doesn't understand. You won't. Yet—I would die'—and I believe that, too. It isn't her fault any more than it is the hyacinth's. They are very much alike. A wonderful flower—and a wonderful woman. I think your wife is the more wonderful of the two—giving you up as she is doing, all because of your work."

Behind her courage was a smoldering depth of pain. Paul thought she looked like an angel as she sat opposite him, with the desk between them—like an exquisite, white-faced nun he had seen in the Ursuline Convent in Quebec. He marveled that she could talk to him like this, trying to soothe a little the wound in his life, when the heart in her own breast was near breaking with its grief. No wonder little children worshiped her and men and women loved her.

"Yes, she is a wonderful woman," he said, thinking only vaguely of his wife. "All women are wonderful. And especially— mothers."

He knew she had come to talk to him about her mother. Carla did not flinch when he brought her mission home to her in this way. She bowed her head a little, then her eyes came back to him with a misty glow in them.

"I don't like to add to your worries," she said. "But it seems necessary. I don't want to go to any other—but you. I think you will help me—a little."

"If my life could save your mother I would give it," said Paul.

His words broke through her calm for a moment.

"I have come to ask if you will take me over to Peribonka to-morrow and help me arrange for a little plot of ground," she said, tightening her hands in her lap. "My mother loves Peribonka. In so many ways it has re-minded her of the village where she was

55

born and from which my father brought her to America. We have dreamed of living there some day, for I love it, too. Now that mother is going to die, she wants to be buried there. To-morrow I want to arrange for a place in the cemetery, as near the river as possible. Mother loves the big, wide river, with its sandbars and birds. She told me to-day just where she would like to rest, in a little corner that was overgrown with wild honeysuckle when we were there last. She is so eager to get it, so happy and smiling and unafraid in planning for it—so wonderful—such a mother—that last night I asked God to let me die and go with her."

Looking into her bravely clear and tear-less eyes, Paul felt himself, for a moment, unable to answer her. Then he said:

"We will go to-morrow, Carla. But it will be a long time before anything happens. It may be—it won't happen at all. Doctors are not infallible. Sometimes——"

56

Carla smiled at him. Her look of gratitude transfigured her face.

"Thank you," she said gently. "It gives me greater courage to know that *you* are hoping for me like that. My mother says the doctors are wrong. That is why I want to go to Peribonka to-morrow. Mother believes she is not going to live through the time they have set for her. She wants to be with me as long as she can, but she insists that the time is very short, much shorter than the doctors have said."

"You believe that?"

"I must." Carla was looking beyond him, as if in the distance were a vision which it would be impossible for him to see. "I try not to believe, but it comes over me and holds me. It isn't just fear."

"I am going to write for Miss Wixom to come and take charge of the children," said Paul. "You must be with your mother without interruption."

Carla drew herself together with a little shock.

"Please don't. I must have the work—the pleasure—the inspiration of the children. Mother wants it that way, too. She sits in her window, and I can see her from the school-house, and we wave our hands at each other every little while. She can see the children, and they are always thinking about her. Even during hours they don't forget. You see, they are as much mother's as mine, and we cannot turn them over to Miss Wixom. It is from children that all of us get our greatest strength and encouragement. They are the April showers in our lives. Mother and I need them."

"You love children," said Paul, and his words were not a question but a thing spoken to himself.

"I worship them. You won't send for Miss Wixom—until it is necessary?"

"No."

As she rose from her chair she took the

picture of Paul's wife from the desk and stood looking at it with her back turned to the light coming through the window. Thus Paul could see them both—the profile of Carla, her exquisitely cut features, the grace and beauty of her head, and his wife smiling up at her out of the picture. After a moment Carla smiled gently in return.

"When is she coming home?" she asked.

"I don't know. She doesn't keep me in touch with her plans. Sometime before Christmas, I think."

He wondered why the note of bitterness persisted in coming into his voice when he spoke of his wife. It annoyed him. He tried to keep it back. Yet it would come out.

"She likes to surprise me," he added, walking around the end of his desk to stand beside Carla. "When the time comes I will get a telegram from her saying she is on board ship or in New York. 'Home, Paul,' she said last time. 'When are you coming to see me?' I wish she loved children as you love them."

"All women love children," replied Carla mysteriously.

"No, she doesn't. I've wanted a lot of them. Boys, mostly. Claire could be such a wonderful mother."

"She will be, some day," said Carla. "I saw the painting of it in her face when she was here, and I see it now—shining in her eyes —in this picture. She has a soul as deep as the sea, Mr. Kirke, and she must love children!"

She replaced the picture on the desk, and Paul helped her again with her raincoat.

"May I go with you?" he asked. "Like the children, I love your mother."

"Oh!"

The word escaped her lips, and the eagerness of it made his heart tingle.

"You mean that? You are not saying it just to be good to me? You love my mother?"

"Yes. Next to my own mother, who has been away from me so long."

He could not understand what he saw in

her face. It was as if a flame had suddenly thrown a glow upon it.

They went out into the rain, and on the narrow cinder path Carla's arm touched Paul's. A soothing and pleasurable sensation accompanied the gentle pressure of it, and he glanced down at her head near his shoulder, imprisoned in its hood. He could see the silken mesh of her long lashes gathering the rain mist.

A few minutes later the mother welcomed him from her chair near the window, from which she could see Carla's school. Carla had taken his hat and coat. A new spirit had entered the house with her. She was smiling, kissed her mother, chirruped a few notes to a bird in a cage as she went for a moment into the kitchen. What a magnificent fight! The cottage was filled with birds and flowers. Out where Carla had gone a canary was singing. A sleepy cat was purring on a cushion at Mrs. Haldan's feet. In a small grate a fire was burning. Contentment and happiness, and not the shadow of death, seemed triumphant about him.

Mrs. Haldan was the soul of this cheer. Twenty-five years in America had taken from her the ruggedness of her native mountains but had left the spirit of their beauty. She looked at Paul with the same eyes that Carla had. Her hair was heavy, like Carla's, and almost white. Her skin was very pale, and smooth as a child's, with the strange, transparent quality about it which Dr. Derwent and his associates had so carefully watched. Paul had a vision of her back in her mountains, a quarter of a century before. How much she must have looked like Carla then! What beauty grew in those out-of-the-way places, like flowers lost in rugged rock crevices, with ages of history and the struggle of life behind it to give it character. A beauty with indestructible memories along with other things. Memory of love, most of all. He knew that Carla's father had died twenty years before, but one could always see him clearly in the eyes of Carla's mother, and when she talked about him it was as though he had gone away on a little visit only yesterday.

Carla would be like that. One love, one man, forever.

There was no pretence in her mother's gladness that he had come. They visited for an hour, and Carla made tea and served little cakes. Mrs. Haldan told pretty incidents about her girlhood—how she had lived on the side of a mountain, with a village and a river so far down in the valley that the river looked like a winding path, and how Carla's father trudged up valiantly every evening to woo her. She told about their wedding, and how they had lived in the village for a time, until the ambition to come to America had seized upon them. Peribonka had brought back vivid pictures of that little village in her homeland.

Never had Paul seen Carla so beautiful as during this wonderful hour he spent with

63

her mother. When he was about to leave, and stood with her alone for a few moments, it seemed to him he could feel the throbbing of her body near him. Her fingers pressed his hand a little convulsively when he said good-bye.

"You have made me happier than I have been in a long time," she said. "I cannot forget it—any more than Mother—has forgotten."

The words repeated themselves in his mind after he had gone. No woman had ever told him that he had made her happy, except his mother. Carla—and his mother. He took a long walk in the rain—up through the jack pines into the heavier evergreen timber, where the drizzle penetrated only in a mist —and the two women walked at his side. Then his wife joined them. Three wonderful women: his mother, Carla, his wife—with a fourth waiting for death back in her chair. The world must forever continue to be beautiful with such women in it. It was Claire,

64

his wife, who turned him about and took him back to Derwent's home. He talked about her that evening. But he said nothing about the other three. They were locked in his heart, and it seemed sacrilege to open the door upon them.

Chapter IV

THE next day was Saturday, and Paul started for Peribonka early in the morning with Carla. Bad weather had given way at last to glorious autumnal sunshine and warmth. He was glad the rain-soaked sand and clay made a horse and buggy necessary. Carla was different, had grown different overnight. The beauty which had come into her face when he was with her mother had not disappeared to leave it so tense and strained again. She seemed nearer to him, infinitely more dependent than yesterday, and happier—if there could be such a thing as that emotion left in her life.

They crossed the great blueberry "burns," with miles and miles of flat, wild country about them, reaching toward the lake on one side and the timbered wilderness on the other. Only at wide intervals was there a habitant's home, and they met no one on the sticky road. Even this barrenness Paul loved. He talked to Carla about the country. All nature, no matter how desolate it might appear to others, was beautiful to him, he said. Nature could not make a desolation that was not beautiful, and never was there a jarring note in its handiwork. Even the stark, charred stubs of burned trees had their place, for drama and tragedy as well as humor and gladness were in Nature's scheme of things, and all were beautiful. Even a pond covered with "frog scum" was like that, a jewel of color made up of a thousand wonders. Because most humans could not see the beauty and pathos of a fire-blackened stub or the enchanting mystery of a dormant pond was not proof that Nature had made an error. It was merely evidence that most human eyes were blind.

In a sandy place he got out and cut bushes weighted heavily with blueberries, and they plucked the luscious fruit from the same stems and ate it as they rode along. It was almost happiness. Only the grim thing shadowing them kept it from being that, and even this shadow seemed to fold its wings for flashing moments. It grew warm, and, with the habit of her mother's people, Carla bared her head to let the air stir in her hair. Paul looked at it, with the restless desire in him growing stronger. It was always so smooth and soft, with its silky coils so gracefully fitting her head, that it seemed a loss of something precious not to touch its beauty. He thought of what Lucy-Belle had told her husband—of the love story in Carla's life. Some man had loved it. Some man had put his hand upon it. As their road came into green timber and he listened to Carla's voice telling him that in her own heart was a love for Nature so great that she would never live in a city again, he wondered what it was that had spoiled her romance so that she would never care for any other man or marry.

They came to Peribonka, and Maria Chapdelaine set them a luncheon in the old-fashioned little dining room overlooking her garden, with its luxuriant array of vegetables and flowers. "If you plant a flower beside a cabbage or a carrot or a beet, the vegetable will do much better," she said to Carla in that sure, sunny way which made the most dolorous grow cheerful in her presence. She admired Carla, and brought in a little girl she had adopted to show her what loveliness one might come to possess if one lived right. Carla was a bit embarrassed, and Paul delighted, by such ardent and frankly spoken approval. Samuel Chapdelaine, tall, thin, and the main prop of Peribonka's church choir, joined them at the table for a visit, and after a time Paul took him aside and explained his mission. They went up the street together, and when they returned the business was over. The small square of ground with its wild honeysuckle vines belonged to Carla.

He took her to see it after they said goodbye to the Chapdelaines, and when they stood over it, looking down at the river, he saw tears in Carla's eyes for the first time since he had known her. She made no movement to hide them or wipe them away when she smiled her gratitude at him. He held out his hand, and she gave him her own. He held it for a few moments, and neither broke the silence which fell between them as they walked down the footworn path and through the picket gate.

An impulse which neither attempted to voice held them for a time in Peribonka. They walked up the springy, broken boardwalk almost to the cheese factory, and then back along the grassy side of the road. They went down to the river's edge and stood where they could see the birds splashing water over themselves on the sandbars. They saw the dumpy little twice-a-week boat from across the lake unloading goods for the villagers and habitants at its dilapidated wharf, and Samuel Chapdelaine waved a hand at them as he hurried down to see if an expected box of freight had arrived. On the opposite shore, close to the wayside, was a shrine. They could see its cross from where they stood, with the sun shining on it. The air was so clear that the tolling of the monastery bells drifted in faintest music to the village, and the frolic and quarrels of the birds on the sandbars came with it.

When they were ready to go Paul felt as if he were leaving something in Peribonka, just as the warmth of Carla's hand had left something in his heart. Carla, Peribonka, the little plot of ground—they would be as unforgettable as Mrs. Haldan's memories. He thought of this as they rode back through the afternoon. He thought of it later when he stood in his office again, and looked down upon the smash and grind of machinery in the pit. It troubled him and made him rest-

Paul felt as if he were leaving something there . . .

less and uneasy. This day, burned deeply into his life, seemed unreal now that it was over. It was as if an experience had turned into a dream, a thing of a few minutes instead of hours.

The friendly, faintly smiling gaze of his wife followed him about the room. He answered her letter that evening, and in his pages to her his freshly roused emotions found their voice. He told about the tragedy in Carla's life, of their journey to Peribonka, and of the little plot of ground in the cemetery. Writing in his office, with his wife's face looking at him, it was not difficult for him to let the floods pour out, just as he had unleashed them once or twice before in his six years of married life with her. He was a man, wanting a woman. He wanted his wife. He did not want her in Europe or Egypt or waiting for him in a palace at home. *He wanted her with him.* He told her this as tenderly as a man could write to a woman. It was a letter of love, of arisen hope, of vision-

77

ings—to his wife. Carla was the inspiration of it.

He sealed and addressed the letter and put it in the company's mail. What a glory life would be if his wife would come at last! He had painted a picture for her in the letter —her golden beauty a part of the blue of open skies, a thing near and wonderful for him to have. But when he went out into the night and looked at the row of lighted cottages on the hill he thought of Carla, and a yearning to be near her possessed him again.

This impulse bewildered him. He went to his bachelor quarters and tried to read. One by one the houses grew dark. Still he endeavored to make his books and magazines interest him. Never had his nerves been more sleeplessly alert, and their obstinacy persisted after he had undressed and gone to bed. He could hear sounds from the pit, the steady *thump, thump, thump* of a spile driver, the gun-like rattle of the riveting machines, the tumult of shunting cars, the everlasting roar and grind of cement drums and rock crushers. These sounds he had heard a thousand nights. It was something else that kept him awake—an incessant stream of things passing through his mind, detached, illogical, unreasonable, and always bringing him back in one way or another to Carla and her mother.

He got up and dressed. It was after midnight. Over the pit hung an illumination which reached up into the sky like the glow from a volcano. He turned down the cinder path and was soon among the men. No one was on the job who did not know him, even in the night shifts. He always seemed like one of them, never swollen with his importance, not afraid to dirty his hands, a friend come down among them to see how things were going. Many of them spoke to him to-night, but their friendliness failed to wipe away the disquiet of mind which had compelled him to get out of bed. He looked at his watch and found it was one o'clock when he reached the far end of the workings. A gravel-made road led to the forest trail higher up, and he took this road out of the pit.

It was a vividly starry night without a moon, and for half an hour he walked briskly until he came to a fork in the trail. One of its branches swung northward toward a sullen, moaning roar, where the Mistassini was driving its mighty forces between ragged islands of rock, the other turned back to the hill. He followed this road.

After a little he came to the row of cottages. There was a light in the Haldan home, and he found himself wondering what Carla did with the long nights in which she waited for the coming of death. Was it possible for her to sleep? Or did she sit alone through dragging hours watching her mother, praying for the day? He stopped at the gate to the picket fence which enclosed her flower gardens, and his ears caught a sound which did not come from the pit. It was like a cry. He

80

opened the gate quietly and went in. A window was open somewhere, and he could hear clearly a voice that was sobbing. It was Carla! No one else in the cottage could be crying like that—surely not Carla's mother. His heart thumped against his ribs. His breath came a little short. He went to the door and knocked against it gently. Then more loudly. Someone came, and the door opened. He entered and stood beside Carla. She had not been in bed, had not undressed. She was as he had left her hours before, except that her face and eyes were stricken with a grief that terrified him. Then, in the dim light, a miracle happened. She smiled at him through tears. *"I was hoping for you,"* she said.

"I was passing—heard you crying——"

He said no more, because he had guessed only half the truth. He was careful to speak so that his voice would not awaken Carla's mother, if she were asleep. His mind was not working quickly, he was bewildered and frightened by the agony in Carla's face, the way she turned and went ahead of him into the big room with Mrs. Haldan's empty chair near the window, and from that to another room that was full of light, and from which the sobbing must have come to him at the gate. In the open door of this room Carla waited, and without turning her head gave him her hand. It was a cold, lifeless little hand, with no spark left of the warmth and thrill which he had felt in it a few hours before. He closed his own over it tightly, for the hand, more than Carla's face and eyes, struck the truth to his heart. They went in. Mrs. Haldan lay in her bed. Her face was lighted with peace, her lips were gently smiling. She was very white and very still. Paul knew she was dead.

Carla drew him nearer. When they were beside her mother she looked up at him. Her eyes, flooded with their pain, were starry bright, almost with pride, almost with glory.

82

"Beautiful," she whispered, the word breaking in her throat.

Paul bowed his head. "Yes, she is beautiful," he said, fighting to keep his voice even.

The hand which was not holding Carla's he placed on her mother's white forehead. For a few moments they stood in this way. Then the same impulse which had drawn his boyish lips to his mother's cold face when her soul was gone made him bend over and kiss the smooth, white brow where his hand had lain. A little cry tore itself from Carla's breast, and freeing her hand from Paul's she sank down upon her knees and pressed her face closely against her mother. For an eternity, it seemed to him, he stood over her —an eternity in which he could find no words for his lips to say, nothing which might help a little to ease the grief which had come so suddenly and crushingly upon her.

Slowly he put out a hand until it rested on Carla's head. Then he gently stroked her hair, and after a little the tenseness went out of Carla's body, and she seemed to be sleeping beside her mother—sleeping with wide-open, misty eyes, which Paul could not see, while through the partly open window came to them the drone and grind and distant tumult of the pit.

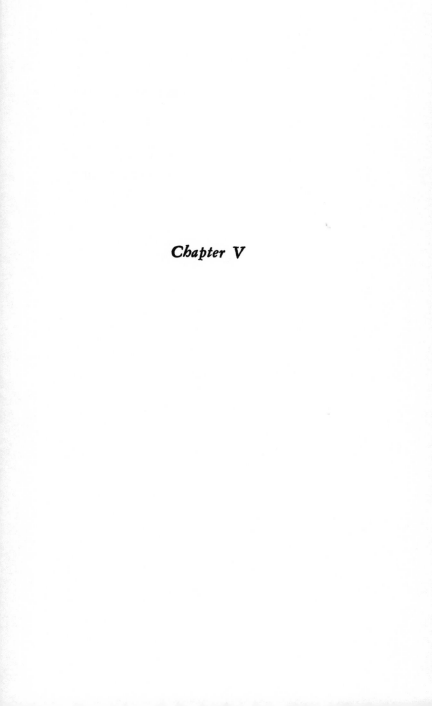

Chapter V

On Tuesday they went to Peribonka.

For thirty minutes there was silence in the pit, the first time in three years. The pit demanded it. It cared nothing for James Kirke, on whose millions it fed, but for Carla Haldan it held a warm affection. Out of the pit came tributes of flowers which smothered the little cottage on the hill, and when Carla and her mother went to Peribonka the soul of the pit went with them. For the first time Paul looked down upon it and almost loved it.

The next day Carla was among her children in the school. This was the most amazing part of her fortitude. Two days later Paul was called unexpectedly to New York.

The new life which submerged him for a fortnight, its passionate business details, its

87

conferences, the talk of still more millions, and of greater activities, was like a plunge into a maelstrom. His father and Durand had perfected a fresh scheme for bringing in another hundred million dollars of other people's money. Each day they were struggling to reach a little farther. Their huge new office building, with its appalling efficiency and ceaseless rush of living creatures, oppressed and dismayed him, and he was startled by its unexpected effect upon him. It was worse than the pit, for the pit had its redeeming edge of wilderness and its human forces at work with their naked hands in rock and clay. Here his mind seemed dulled, his wits blunted, his senses overwhelmed by the magnitude of the things which he knew were happening without the physical use of hands and bodies, without the flesh and blood vigor—the strain of brawn and muscle—which had made the pit endurable for him. He made no great effort to enter into it or to understand it. The house where his mother had lived seemed no longer even the husk of a home. He spent only a part of one day in his own home, where Claire would be on her return from Europe. It was filled with a cathedral stillness, wrapped up, packed away, moth-protected, like a palace whose occupants had suddenly died, a place guarded by soft-footed and obsequious servants who made him shiver. It was a sepulcher of hopes for him, a place of gayety and laughter and entertainment for Claire. Here he felt about him a clinging emptiness, a great loneliness, a haunting unrest—and in this same environment Claire would find amusement and happiness when she returned. The truth of the thing added to his heaviness of heart. A new note had come into his thoughts. He was beginning to ask himself if Claire, with all her wealth and freedom, were really happy. And if, in any way, it were possible for him to make her happy.

He had written to her immediately after the death of Carla's mother, and toward the end of the fortnight he sent her another letter. He had the desire to write more frequently than he did, but some subtle force crept between him and the performance of the act. He wanted her more than ever, and in this last letter, his third since he had heard from her, he told of the loneliness of the great house, its emptiness, its coldness, and how only her golden presence could bring it back to life. Inspirationally he made a suggestion. If she would come back and spend only a little while with him upon the Mistassini, he would take her anywhere she might want to go when the job was off his hands—around the world, if that would please her. It would be rather wonderful, wouldn't it? Around the world—just they two! He asked the question with almost boyish hope and earnestness.

He was glad when the day arrived for him to leave for the Mistassini, for there seemed to be something of homeness about the pit for him now. The company boat met him at

Roberval, across the lake. When he first caught the gleam of sunlight on the white, bare walls of the monastery at the mouth of the Peribonka, he felt as if a soothing and friendly influence had come to possess him. He watched them until they were shut out by a headland between them and the Mistassini, and then he figured out a spot in the sky, beyond the screen of forest, under which Peribonka must lie. He would go there often, he thought, and would take Claire with him when she came.

A press of business awaited him at his office, and not until the day after his return did he see Carla. She was among her children, in the closing hour of school in the afternoon. The tragic strain which he had observed in her face before her mother's death had disappeared. A deeper and more permanent thing had taken its place, and though it was less poignant, it stirred him for a moment with a sensation of uneasiness, as if he had personally lost something. He could not

91

tell just what it was, then or afterward. She seemed older, as if he had been away two years instead of two weeks, and he felt, in an unaccountable way, as if a distance as wide as the pit itself had come between them. Even the little tremble of gladness in her voice when she greeted him did not dispel this effect.

He walked with her to the cottage, and she showed him what the early frosts had done to her nasturtiums and asters. "I won't be able to send you many more," she told him.

She gave him flowers for his office, and when he returned with them and put them on his desk, he was oppressed still more by the sense of having missed an important and necessary thing which he had expected to find when he came back to the pit. He was sure that Carla had been glad to see him. But she was not the same Carla he had taken over the blueberry plains to Peribonka. He doubted if she would personally come to his office with flowers again.

In this he was mistaken. She came on Saturday morning with an armful of asters. Another night or two of frost and they would all be gone, she said. She asked about Claire, and they talked for a few minutes of his visit to the city. She did not speak of her mother, or Peribonka, or anything that had to do with herself—except her flowers and her school. As she arranged the flowers she bent over his desk so that the silky head which he had stroked with his hand was very near him, and suddenly he felt himself overwhelmed by a flame that left no part of him untouched. When Carla's deft fingers finished their task, she found Paul looking at her with a face that was wholly Indian once more. He thanked her as he might have thanked her a year ago. His hand touched hers for just a moment, and a swift throb came in Carla's throat. Their eyes met, Carla's faultlessly clear and pure and filled

93

with a shining light—Paul's with a somber, settled grimness far back in them.

At his door they paused another moment. Then Carla left him.

It was her last visit to his office.

Within an hour after she had gone Paul was driving to Peribonka alone. The roads had hardened, and he made it quickly in his car. The asters and a bunch of roses which had come to him from Roberval he placed on Mrs. Haldan's grave. Carla had been there, for the grave was well cared for and covered with flowers from her garden, most of them faded and shriveled by the frosts. These he gathered in a cluster and placed in a pot by themselves, near his roses. He remembered that Carla loved flowers even when their colour and life were gone.

He made no effort to blind himself to the fact which had leaped upon him so irresistibly when he had looked at Carla's head bent over his desk. The futility of such evasion struck him with almost equal force. He

The silky head was very near him, and suddenly he felt himself overwhelmed by a flame.

wanted Carla, and that want was as much a part of him as his vision or his sense of the obligations of life. It was she who had brought him back to the Mistassini with a feeling that he was on his way home. His regard for her was not a sudden irruption brought about by a physical or emotional restlessness, which might have been stirred by her nearness and her beauty. He could look back and see where it had been growing in him slowly over a period of three years, so slowly that it had not been difficult for him to escape its true significance. But now there was no longer the possibility of either avoidance or self-deception. He knew that Carla meant more to him than friendship, and that only a miracle had held his arms from taking her into them.

He also believed that a flash of understanding had come into her eyes when she looked at him and saw in his face the grim shadowing of the fight which from that moment he was bound to make.

After this Paul was more than ever filled with the desire to go among the men and work with his hands, and he was seldom in his office. Every muscle in his body yearned for the strenuous activity of work which he saw piled upon others, and he let down the bars which his position had compelled him to accept, until, at times, one coming upon him in the pit would have taken him for a laborer. He was skillful with the ax, and one day late in October he had finished hewing a saddle into a heavy timber when he turned about to find Carla standing a few feet away, looking at him. She had come to the far edge of the pit to find the father of one of her boys, and for a moment it seemed to Paul that he caught in her face a look which bridged in a few seconds the abysmal gulf which he had felt growing between them since her mother's death. He went to her, breathing quickly because of his exertions, and Carla laughed softly, almost with a lit-

tle triumph in her throat, when he showed
her his hands blackened by pine pitch.

He went to Peribonka frequently during
these autumn days, and once a week he had
flowers sent to him from Roberval for Mrs.
Haldan's grave. Carla knew of his visits to
the little cemetery, and Paul made no effort
to conceal them from her. He never went on
Sunday, which was Carla's day with her
mother. When she tried to express to him the
depth of her gratitude, he talked as if it
were the spirit of his own mother he was
thinking of when he took flowers to Peribonka. But he felt he was not hiding the
truth from her, and was rather glad of it. It
was a satisfaction for him to know that
Carla was conscious of his thoughts about
her. It made his fight easier, gave it a certain
thrill, which comes to a man when he is
aware that someone he cares for is watching
him. And the knowledge of it could not
harm Carla, in whose life another love had
fastened itself so securely that no corner of

99

her heart could be filled with an emotion responsive to his own. They made no effort to avoid each other, except that he did not take her to Peribonka and she did not come to his office any more, and one day when they were together he asked her frankly why she did not marry. No sooner were the words spoken than he was sorry. He could see the hurt flame up for an instant in her eyes, like a fire from which a curtain had been suddenly snatched away; and then it died out, leaving her face a little whiter, but smiling at him gently, as if she were apologizing for letting it affect her in that way. Then she told him. It was almost traditional in their family that a woman should have but one love. And she had loved a man, still loved him, with all her heart and soul, though he was gone from her forever. The love had come into her life a long time ago. She emphasized this fact, gazing away from him with her long lashes veiling eyes filled with mystic visions.

100

He was glad he had heard the words from her own lips. It built up a new comradeship between them and made him more positive of his triumph over himself. A letter from Claire helped him. His wife laughed at him pleasantly for his whimsical suggestion of a journey around the world, and then painted in her picturesque and vivid way the torture which she knew such a trip would be for him. *"Without your forests, your open skies, your big outdoors, you would die before we got half around, Paul,"* she wrote him. *"It would be merciless of me to make you pay in that way for my presence up at the Mistassini. I am coming, and just because I want to come. I am anticipating seeing something very wonderful up there, something which will mean greatly more to you and me than six months or a year rambling around the earth. As for such a trip, with* you *in it"*—and then she went on to tell him more about himself than he thought she had ever known. The letter thrilled him. It gave him a new vision of Claire, who had never analyzed him in this gentle and understanding way, portraying for him the life which he loved as though it were a part of herself. But in the end, after assuring him again that she was coming to him and was looking forward to the time when they would be together, she said her return to America might be postponed until the following May or June. Could he wait that long?

Carla also received a letter from Claire. It was filled with a womanly tenderness and sympathy for one who had suffered a great loss, and was filled with the intimate knowledge and sentiment which could only have been given and inspired by Paul. Carla let him read it. Her eyes were strangely alight, though she had prepared herself to show it to him.

"You told me once that millions could not buy sentiment," she said. "And millions could not bring what has come in her letter. It is her heart speaking to me."

102

Carla became so deeply absorbed in work outside of her school that he did not talk with her again for a week. She formed evening classes, in which she taught English to the adults who wanted to come to them, and the few spare hours of her afternoons were spent among the mothers of her school children. With the coming of winter Paul buried himself more passionately in the actual stress of outdoor labor, leaving his office routine largely to others, and the change benefited him. Carla, on the other hand, seemed to have assumed too great a burden. The strain, if it were that, began to show its effect on her, until Lucy-Belle noted it and remonstrated with Paul.

"Every day she is growing less like the Carla we knew before her mother died," she told him. "She is breaking under an effort to keep her mind away from herself. Yesterday I dropped into her cottage for a moment when I knew she was there, and I found her crying. She is growing paler, and it frightens me to see the loveliness fading slowly out of her face. You must do something, Paul, make her drop her night classes, send her away for a vacation if you can. I think I am the only one she confides in at all, and I should not betray her confidence—not even what I have guessed about her. But something is eating at her life which isn't entirely the loss of her mother. She insists that her night work is a pleasure, says she is feeling well and doesn't want to go away. But I know of a dream she has always had of visiting her mother's country. If the company could arrange something like that——"

Paul saw Carla the next day, a cold Sunday with snow on the ground. For the first time in many weeks they had a long walk together, and at the beginning of it she settled any suggestions he might have had in his mind. It was as if she saw written in his face what Lucy-Belle had said to him. She mentioned Mrs. Derwent's visit and told him what she had said about her work, smiling the other's fears away as absurd and without reason, and adding with a very decisive little note in her voice that to give up this work or go away, as Lucy-Belle had suggested, was the last thing she would think of doing.

She had heard again from his wife. It was her third letter, and came from Capri, where she was spending the winter, painting. Claire had sent her a little sketch of the vineyards and the picturesque houses on their rock cliffs. These letters, Carla said, would always remain brightly in her memories, they were so friendly and cheering. She had answered them, and had tried to tell Claire a little about her own work, and of the glory and beauty of the great forests and mighty rivers near them. But she lacked the creative soul which his wife possessed, and could not adequately describe them.

Paul knew that something of Carla's real soul was gone even as she talked to him.

His own dragged heavily through the winter. Spring came, and his days at the pit were almost over. August would see his work finished. He did not know what he would do then, he told Carla. Things were happening in South America. He might go there. Carla's future was settled for another year. The government had offered her a contract to remain with the children on the Mistassini, and she had accepted. She hoped that within a year or two she might be able to find a place in Peribonka, near her mother.

Late in May Paul's wife sailed from Cherbourg on the *Empress of France* and, to his surprise, was coming straight to Quebec to join him.

"That is wonderful of her," said Carla, her eyes shining with the light which was always in them when she was thinking or speaking of Claire. "She is coming directly to you!"

The day he left for Quebec he saw her for a few moments to say good-bye.

"I wish I were a man—*and you*," she said.

A radiance was in her face when he left her.

That evening, at dinner, Lucy-Belle said to her husband: "Carla's school was closed this afternoon. Beryl told me she dismissed the children because she had a headache. We must go over and see her."

"I have been there," replied Derwent. "I was a bit worried when one of the boys told me what had happened, so I went over to see if she needed me, and found her—crying."

"Oh!" exclaimed Lucy-Belle. "Now I think I understand!"

She said nothing more to her husband about Carla Haldan.

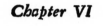
Chapter VI

THE crowning point of anticipation in Paul's six years of married life was his journey to meet Claire. From the Mistassini to Roberval, from Roberval to Metebechewan, and from there down to Chicoutimi, where he took the cross-wilderness train to Quebec, he built steadily to the visions which the increasing interest and comradeship in his wife's letters had helped him to create during the long winter. That she was not following her usual precedent of going to New York, but was coming to him, gave him an emotional thrill which it had not previously been his happiness to experience in his relationship with her. He believed that for Claire to divert herself in this way from home, her own people, and a host of friends after an absence of nearly a year, that she might come to him in a wilderness which she frankly detested, was almost dramatically significant of a change in her attitude toward him. It was the mystery of his change which withheld from his feeling the one thing which might have made it a real passion of expectancy and joy. In none of her letters, which had drawn her nearer to him than she had ever been, had she spoken of love. Even in response to the warmest of his communications to her she had given him no definite satisfaction, except to write him in a way which, without openly avowing herself, drew her closer to him, and gave to his ideals of her a glowing, fleshly reality which excited and possessed him as he went to meet her.

He had a night in Quebec before the *Empress of France* arrived. It was a restless, almost sleepless night, and he walked much of the time through the quaint streets of the town. It was here he could not keep Carla out of his mind. She came to him vividly when he stood in the shadow of the ancient chapel of the Ursulines, where he had seen through the chancel grating the lovely nun whose face and eyes had looked so much like Carla's. In Lower Town he went into the little old church of Notre Dame des Victoires, and he felt as if she were standing at his side. She seemed to be a part of the composure and beauty and age-old enchantment of these quaint and hallowed spots which he loved, as if in some past day her soul had helped to mold and fit their destinies. Here, like himself, Carla could dream, and see ghosts and mystic fabrics of forgotten things where others saw only slow dissolution and ruin of brick and mortar and wood. In her eyes were the deep and slumbering lights which linked the memories of the past with the mysteries of the future—in Claire's the vibrant life of a glorious present. Together, he thought, these two women held the world in their breasts, from its beginning to its end.

He was at the Canadian Pacific Steamship dock an hour ahead of the ship. When it arrived he drew himself back of the waiting people, for he knew that Claire would not be in the rush of disembarking passengers, nor would she be along the rail in the crush that always gathered to wave their greetings to friends and relatives. It surprised him when he found her to be one of the first on the landing walk. As she came down he could see that she was looking for him. She was the same Claire, tall, slim, exquisitely dressed, a woman to be picked out of a thousand. He could always expect Claire like that, a wife any man would be enormously proud to possess. He waved his hat, and she saw him. A swift, beautiful smile passed over her face, and in his eagerness to reach her he made his way a little roughly through the crowd. His heart was jumping. He was meeting her alone —no one but himself to greet her, while always before there had been many. One dream had come true!

When they met he held out his arms. But that was not Claire's way. She was always

right, never forgetful of the fitness of things
—and gave him her hands. Her fingers closed
warmly about his. She raised her lips and
kissed him, with the light touch of her mouth
which was a part of Claire.

"Dear old Paul!" she said. "At last I'm
home!"

Three days after her arrival in Quebec
Claire was mistress of the bungalow which
her husband had prepared for her visit.
Thereafter Paul could look from the window of his office to the physical realization
of the second of his dreams. Claire was at
last one of the wives who lived in the row
of cottages on the hill. While this dream,
like the friendly but dispassionate greeting
of his wife in Quebec, missed something in
its fulfilment, it had opened doors through
which he was looking to still greater things
for himself, and the woman who was making
this fight against prejudice and environment
for him.

"This time I am going to stay until you become tired of me and send me home," she told him.

The change in her was inexplicable, unless he accepted it as one of sheer sportsmanship. This he did, and was warmed by the thought of what he was bound to give in return for it. Behind her effort it was not difficult for him to see the truth—her struggle against instincts and impulses as deeply inborn as was his own Indian blood in himself. The desire to please him, its sunny cheer and friendliness, was an inspiration to him and strengthened his resolution to twist and bend his life, so that it would fit in with hers. He did not tell her this. The thought of explaining to her that he was about to make a mighty endeavor to cross the gulf which lay between them was embarrassing to him. Claire had said nothing about her own effort. Her actions had shown him the way. This lack of intimacy between them at times made him feel scarcely closer to her than some of the

116

many friends she had. It was a thing which he could not tear down even in moments when some impulse or situation seemed to draw them very close together. He knew that Claire felt it as well as himself. Facing it, smiling at each other, waiting for some force greater than themselves to break the way for them, they said nothing about it. Each was hoping, and struggling, that this thing between them might be triumphed over. But it persisted in spite of them.

Each day he found something new and unexpected in Claire to increase his admiration for her. She became acquainted with the pit. She put on rubber boots and explored its muddy depths with him. She made no discrimination among his friends, and nodded and smiled as pleasantly at a foreman or a laborer as she did at the others on the hill. More puzzling to him than these things was her intimacy with Carla Haldan. After her first few days on the Mistassini they were together much of the time when Carla was not at her work. Even in this Claire joined her now and then, and talked to the children in Carla's classes about the boys and girls in other lands, and came to know their mothers, until she began to fill a little of Carla's place among them.

Carla came to his office again, but always with Claire. She was unlike the Carla who had brought him flowers, so different from her that he was left with a dully painful sense of loss when he was alone and thinking about her, as if someone very dear to him had died, leaving only memories behind. The paradoxical reason for this emotion in him was that Carla appeared to be strangely and forgetfully happy. The quiet, wonderful depths in her eyes, with their hidden pools and changing shadows of thought, were no longer there. She was lively and gay, and joined freely in the small social affairs of the camp from which she had always held herself more or less apart. She talked only a little of Peribonka, and the forests, and of the places

They were together much of the time . . .

which he knew she loved, but seemed to hold her heart when listening to Claire's colorful descriptions of interesting places his wife had visited. The two had a real affection for each other. No matter how uncertainty might cloud his judgment in other ways, there could be no doubt about this sentiment of mutual regard which had grown up quickly between them.

One evening Claire said to him:

"It is strange how deeply I care for Carla. There is something about her which drags me out of myself, to her. Yet I am finding it more and more impossible to paint her as I want her, she is so completely changed. Where is the real Carla, Paul? What has happened to her? Do you know?"

Her head was bowed over a bit of lacework in her lap, and she did not look at Paul.

"I have noticed the change in her," he said. "It has happened since you came. I think you have helped to bring her out of the terrible grief which oppressed her after her mother's death."

Claire smiled gently at her husband. For a few moments a contemplative light lay in her eyes, as if she were looking—not at him —but at a child.

"You think she is happier—since I came?"

"There is no doubt of it," he declared.

"But I cannot paint her. And it is because—there is so much unhappiness behind what she is trying to make us see in her face."

In his puzzled silence, she added:

"I am wondering why she tries so hard to make *me* believe she is happy, Paul."

Before he could answer she began to tell him about her talk to the children in Carla's school that day.

Chapter VII

CLAIRE came to the Mistassini on the first of June. It was the fifteenth when they went to what Paul called the Big Gorge, ten miles back in the rocky forests. This is the date which will remain a long time on the calendars of the simple-hearted folk north of Lac St. Jean, because of the miracle which happened on it. It is a date almost to be canonized. Priests speak of it, and people point it out, as a day of infallible proof of the omnipotence of God.

Lucy-Belle is not remembered, though it was she who planned the expedition to the gorge. In it, besides herself, were her husband and Paul, Claire and Carla. For two days preceding the journey Paul had men on the rough and narrow trail clearing it of obstructions and overhanging limbs and brush so that they might travel over it on horseback.

Paul had seen Claire turn white and tremble at the foaming unrest of the Mistassini beating eternally against its rocks, just as he had felt her shiver, one evening, in a deep and gloomy place in the forest, where the wind was whistling through the pine tops over their heads. He had taken her hand, and her fingers had clung tightly to his, as if these things which he loved sent a horror through her. On the morning of this eventful fifteenth of June, with sunshine and birds about them, he and Derwent rode a little behind their wives and Carla, and never had Claire looked so lovely to him. Her beautiful body seemed vibrant with the thrill of the day, her voice was sweet to hear, her eyes were filled with laughter, until he could almost make himself believe she loved the things which she was facing, and which had so completely conquered her until now. Her unhatted golden head and Carla's dark one rode side by side, one a shining radiance in the sun, the other richly lustrous, with gleamy pools and seas of darker shadow in it. For half a mile they followed a trail so close to the river that its roaring tumult drowned their voices and cobwebby drifts of spray came to wet their faces. Through this Paul rode close to the side of his wife, and saw her smile and fight to hide its effect upon her. Then they struck Indian file into the narrow, rocky, deeply rooted trail to the gorge, with Paul at the head of the little procession and Derwent following last. Occasionally the trail widened so that Paul could drop back and ride beside Claire, and each time he noted a little more in her face and eyes the thing she was fighting against, her dislike of the black forests and the earthly smelling swamps and the rocky fragments of hills they were traveling through.

Toward mid-afternoon they came to the Big Gorge. Those who have seen it can never forget the spectacle of its thundering water tearing itself out of a finger of the cavernous

Laurentians, crashing through the open for a space in whirling maelstroms, then narrowing into a sullen, oily-looking avalanche of irresistible force as it descends into a chasm whose rock walls become higher and closer, until, at last, its fury and voice disappear again into the bowels of the Laurentians, making the earth tremble with its subterranean rumble and roar.

Its effect on Claire was not what Paul had anticipated. To his amazement it was she who suggested they spread their luncheon on the edge of a great slab of rock which projected into the stream, and from where they could look upon the wonderful play of water below them. This rock, several acres in extent, was covered with soil which was continually absorbing moisture from the river, so that it had clothed itself with a carpet of flowers and grass until it was an oasis of beauty in the heart of a rock-visaged landscape which otherwise would have possessed little to offset its more forbidding aspects. It

128

was Claire who also selected the spot for their tablecloth and who arranged their places afterward so that all might sit looking toward the mouth of the overhung chasm, several hundred yards downstream from the rock which held its tenure like an indomitable guardian before it. Between their position and the abyss of the gorge was a black and irresistible sweep of water which had the appearance of a flood of boiling oil on its way to the mouth of a huge funnel. Halfway to the orifice a rock slowly wearing away with the centuries reared its grim and battered head out of the stream, cutting it like a knife in two equal parts. Even about this jagged tooth of stone was no glint of sunlit whiteness of froth or foam, and no sound came from this part of the channel except a sullen murmur and hiss, lending still greater reality to the caprice of thought that water must metamorphose itself to oil before the throat of the gorge would receive it. It was from the other side of the table-rock that the chief tumult came, where for half a mile or more the huge churns of the river bed were at work, slashing and twisting the down-rushing floods until, Paul thought, they were an inspiring and beautiful thing to look upon.

Yet it was the darker and more sinister side that Claire chose, with a scene under their eyes that was colossally awesome but equally unbeautiful.

As they ate their luncheon she let him know, for the first time, something of the strange fear which possessed her whenever she was near the fury of rushing water. He was surprised she should speak of it now, and not at some time when they had been alone. Derwent roused the confusion in her by saying, in answer to a question asked by Carla, that no living creature whose habitat was land could exist for more than a few seconds in the oily Charybdis below them.

Claire shrugged her slim shoulders and looked with unafraid eyes upon what Derwent had accredited with the omnipotence of superdestruction.

"Were you ever haunted by a dream?" she asked. "I have been, since childhood. Most children dream of falling from ladders and housetops, of seeing ghosts, of running away from dangers—but mine was always of water. It has remained with me. I am terribly afraid of water, but only when it is angry. The ocean terrifies me when it lashes itself white. I found a lovely place to paint in Cornwall, but the surf was always beating against the cliffs and drove me away. Water like this below us does not disturb me at all. It is so smooth and unbroken, like the ripples in Carla's hair when it is down—so soft and velvety looking as it turns over and over that I can scarcely believe what you have said, Dr. Derwent. I would jump into it without fear, while back there—where it is breaking itself into spray and foam—I would never have the courage to start!"

"There you might live—here there could be no possibility of it," said Derwent.

"I can almost fancy walking upon it without wetting my shoes, it is so firm and substantial looking," persisted Claire.

"Did you ever stand on a mountain top and look down into the clouds and think how nice it would be to jump off into one of the cozy little nests they make?" asked Lucy-Belle. "I have. Once I think I might have done it if Colin hadn't held me. He says I would have had another mile to go after I hit the cloud. But this down here doesn't appeal to me like a nice, white cloud all filled with feathers. It makes me think of a —a big boa constrictor running into a hole! I wouldn't try to walk on it, or jump into it, unless Colin fell in first and I had to help him."

"Would you—then?" asked Paul.

Lucy-Belle meditated for a moment.

"Of course I would," she said. "Do you

132

suppose I would let him go into that tunnel alone?"

"I—wonder. Life is a precious thing. In ninety-nine cases out of a hundred it is more precious than the person we live with. We don't idealize the women who burn themselves on their husbands' funeral pyres in India. Do we?"

"I don't think so. Their sacrifice was inspired by duty and a religious faith. Neither takes the place of love. But if Colin were down there, going to a death like that, I would want to go with him. I *would* go. I cannot explain it. Isn't there a difference?"

"Yes—a difference that is infinite," said Claire. "In this instance a woman would be joining the man she loved in a final hour of life, that they might be together in the supreme moment. It would be choosing between a few more minutes *with* him or a few more years *without* him, and minutes measured by love are more priceless to a woman than years without it."

133

"Also to a man," said Derwent, holding his wife's hand closely for a moment. "I don't think we would hesitate to take the leap. Do you, Paul?"

"No."

He was looking at Carla, who was gazing meditatively upon the viscous sweep of water below them. She looked up almost in the moment his glance went to her. Her lips moved, as if for an instant she were on the point of speaking to him, and to him alone. Then she caught herself, and turned her gaze to the river again.

"A woman's love for a man isn't always like that," she said, and something in her voice strangely thrilled Paul. "I think there is a love so great that it is cowardly for it to deliberately die, a love so complete that when its other half goes there is still heaven left in memories of it. It is wicked to take the breath of human life from such a love because of a selfish desire not to live alone. I think, Lucy-Belle, if it came to the real test

134

God would give you strength to hold yourself back. You would not die. You would live, and cherish the memories of your love like a garden of beautiful flowers."

It was as if a cathedral bell had tolled softly among them, so wonderfully gentle and strange was Carla's voice. *Carla knew.* That was the thought which gripped Paul, and it held the others. She had passed through the fire at which his wife and Lucy-Belle were only guessing, and it was from her soul, not her lips, that evidence had come. Claire gave a little start at his side, and her face and eyes grew suddenly and vividly filled with light as she looked at Carla, as if all in a second a great and half-expected truth had come to possess her. Stranger even than the change in her face was the way in which she found Paul's hand and held it tenderly and warmly between her own. Never had the thrill of her entered into him as during these moments. He closed his hands tightly about hers. *But be was looking at Carla.*

Lucy-Belle sprang to her feet and drew Derwent after her.

"Let's not get sentimental!" she cried. "I'm going to throw all kinds of things down to my boa constrictor and see what he does with them. This to begin with——" and she flung out a paper plate which curved and circled, until, lighting gracefully upon the surface of the torrent below, it was caught like a feather and whipped with the speed of a bullet toward the maw of the gorge, without so much as getting its inner side wet.

Claire gave a gasp of amazement.

"I did not dream the water sped as swiftly as that!" she exclaimed. "But see! It is as I said! The plate is going—it has disappeared into the tunnel—and not once was it ruffled or upset. Back where the water is breaking and roaring it would have been destroyed."

"Wait!" said Derwent. He rolled the short log which they had used for a seat to the edge of the cliff, and with Paul's help tilted

136

it on end and flung it over. "There goes a man," he laughed. "Now see what happens!"

They stood close to the sheer edge of the table-rock and saw the log as it struck the water. There was an oily splash, and for a few yards the wood drifted away as smoothly as the plate had gone. A smile of triumph curved Claire's lips, then swiftly a frightened look gathered in its place. A hand had reached up, a terrible, unseen hand that had gripped the log like a living thing and dragged it down until no chip or shadow of it rode the liquid serpent under them.

"Hold your eyes near the rock!" commanded Derwent.

Breathlessly they watched. Half a minute later, as if spewed up by the monster who had swallowed it, the log reappeared near the huge fang which split the stream, struck against it, and climbed half its length out of the water, then sank back and disappeared again, this time to be seen no more.

"Gone," said Derwent. "And if you stood

137

at the other end of the gorge five or six miles from here, you would never see that log come through. It is ground to pieces, goes out of existence in whatever there is between the walls of the chasm, which no man has ever explored, and none ever will. Are you satisfied?"

Claire was staring, wide-eyed.

"I believe it—now," she said.

Lucy-Belle had turned a little white.

"Still—I would jump in," she maintained, looking at Derwent.

Again Paul looked at Carla. The calm and placid beauty of her face seemed accentuated by what they had seen.

"And the wonder of it is there are so many who believe that Nature and God are not One!" she said, only for him. "Is it possible that in the blindness of our egoism we shall always fail to understand the significance of such things as *that?*" It is a written word, in the hand of God, just as the Peribonka, with its gentleness and sunshine, is another and different message for us. That is what I believe."

Paul nodded. "So do I," he said, and felt the desire of all the world to take Carla's head against his breast and hold it there.

Guilt fastened itself upon him, and a little later, inspired by the sweetness of her manner toward him, he whispered to his wife: "Claire, you are wonderful! God knows I hope some day to make you happy!"

"You will," she answered, and the gentle mystery in her voice and eyes stirred him with a deep emotion.

Until the play grew tiresome they brought sticks and chunks of wood from the edge of the timber and fed them to the hidden hands of the stream. The result was always the same, except that chips and grass and very light pieces of wood raced swiftly and safely away, like the pasteboard plate, as if they were too insignificant to attract attention from below. But with the heavier objects there was a variation so small in what happened that the watchers on the rock were amazed and fascinated, and started a little game of guessing how many seconds would pass before Lucy-Belle's huge snake spat up an object and then swallowed it again.

To end their sport Paul and Derwent staggered from the edge of the timber with a forty-foot log, which had lain so long in the drying sun and wind that they could bear its weight on their shoulders, and before this was tossed over the five made their guesses, the loser to entertain the other four at dinner the next day.

"I've a notion to ride this log through the gorge!" exclaimed Lucy-Belle. "I want to know what is under and between those walls which you say no one has ever explored, Colin. What do you suppose can be there?"

"An inferno of devils, I imagine," replied her husband.

"Possibly not. Fairies might live there," suggested Claire.

"A black and sunless place where lovely
140

water maids without eyes frolic in the darkness," added Paul.

"Or a Kingdom of Micomicon, where dreams are made and sent out into the world," said Carla.

Derwent was preparing his end of the log for a final heave. "I insist it is a place of devils and death. Still, like Lucy-Belle, I'd like to see what's there. After all, it's fifty million years of—mystery! Are you ready, Paul?"

"Ready!"

The log pitched down, and as it went the end of it swung like a living thing and struck Paul. Even before the blow—in the lightning flash of time when eyes behind could see it sweeping upon him—a sudden scream filled his consciousness, and as the timber caught him he saw it was Claire whose cry had tried to warn him. Then he was over. With photographic clearness his eyes beheld his fate. The water seemed to reach up and catch him on its oily breast, and for a brief instant after this there was a sensation not unpleasing about its hold. For some unaccountable reason he felt no sense of fear or terror even when forces that were irresistible but gentle pulled him down. He knew it was death, the death they had played with and lightly talked about, yet its presence closing about him did not rob his mind of its vision and judgment, nor frighten him into senseless wrestling with it. He would come up again, alive, near the jagged tooth of rock; after that would be his end, and in such an hour as this seconds became eternities of life. His wife, Carla, Lucy-Belle, and Derwent were still nearer to him than the final stroke of death; he would see them, especially Claire and Carla, when he looked back in those few moments of grace which the monsters of the undertows would give him. These two, and the supreme faith which had wrought a comradeship between him and all the forces of Nature, gave him, instinctively and without effort, the courage not to be afraid.

The undercurrent's indraughts and refluxes carried him with a quiet and deliberate leisureliness, which gave him no physical discomfort except that of holding his breath. Yet they were so powerful, so utterly sure in their grip, that when he made an experimental effort to reach the surface it was as if he were struggling against a wooden wall. To save the air in his lungs he restrained himself from further exertion, and when, at last, he came up near the rock, and felt fresh air in his face, he had suffered no greater inconvenience than if he had taken a long dive. His first thought was of the log, his second of the granite snag. Against this, after a moment, he felt himself being slowly lifted, and throwing out his hands he was thrilled by the fibrous, slimy touch of a rope-like substance which had gathered thickly about it just under the surface of the water. River weeds and flag had wrapped themselves in a tough belt about the rock, and so firmly had they attached themselves to it that he knew they would, for a time at least, hold up his weight

143

from the sucking undertow which was already beginning to drag at his limbs.

He looked toward the cliff and raised one hand to wave at the four who stood there. With the distance, and the water in his eyes, he could not make out which was Claire or Carla or Lucy-Belle. But something told him it was his wife who stood nearest to the edge, with her arms reaching out toward him.

And then, on the cliff, one woman said to another: "Are you going with him?"

The woman spoken to gazed wide-eyed—motionless—voiceless—and after a moment of tense waiting the other said: "Then—I am!"

Chapter VIII

PAUL saw the swift, deliberate plunge through space of the slim body, which, in the uncertainty of his vision, an instinctive and positive impulse told him was Claire's. A woman's piercing cry came from the cliff, but no responsive echo of horror escaped his own lips, no sound, but an inarticulate gasp as the figure struck the water and disappeared. An appalling and devastating weakness seized upon him, a deadly sickness of shock, a thing that loosened the grip of his fingers from the clinging belt of weeds and made him limply impotent against the dragging force of the undertow. For an instant his brain reeled in darkness. He began to go down, easily and slowly, as if the cruel and murderous hands below were fearful of arousing him from the inertness to which he had momentarily succumbed. Then water struck into his face and startled him. Heart and brain leaped in response to its warning, and he thrust up wildly and caught the weeds again. They hung closely to the rocks, allowing him to drag his body up until his shoulders were out of water once more. He heard Derwent shout, as if from a mile away, but he paid no attention to the cry, nor did he look toward the cliff. The thought in his mind was that Claire would be with him in another moment or two. She would come to the surface near the rock, and he must be ready to seize and hold her with him until the weeds gave way—or a miracle happened.

Five or six feet from him, where the water was like a pool of oil that had no motion, a little disturbance suddenly flecked its surface—a change of light, a drifting up of something intangible and shadowy, a nebulous blotch which changed under his eyes to substance, a floating mass of hair. The sun was shining, the water was almost black, but

He swung himself out, thrusting against the rock . . .

there was no glint of gold in what he saw. The hair was dark. Carla's face became a part of it in a moment. It seemed to him that the monsters who lived about the rock held her up for him, with a smile on her lips and in her eyes, her face toward him and her arms reaching out. He was half in a daze, and might have fancied some of the things he saw. But Carla was there. She, not his wife, had come to join him in death. The quiet, terrible drama of it held him from calling her name as he waited for her to come within his reach. But the undertow brought her no nearer. For a second, two of them, three or four, it held her away from him, and each of these seconds was a lifetime in passing. Then he saw the distance between them widening, and as it widened the things below began to drag Carla down. She made no struggle, did not cry out to him, but only raised her hands so that he might see they were waiting for him, and wanting him, as she went to her Kingdom of Micomicon, her land of dreams.

He swung himself out, thrusting against the rock, and when the ogres of the water pit dragged at their victims Carla was in his arms. His brain was keenly alive again, and he knew that teams of oxen could have pulled but futilely against the undercurrents, which, one after another, were transporting them irresistibly and yet without great haste through watery space. Thought of physical salvation scarcely filtered in a ray of hope through his mind, and his senses were unterrified by the suffocating presence of death. In Carla were his strength and courage. He locked his arms about her closely. He could feel her clinging to him with the same desire to remain inseparable when the end came. Strange. A Kingdom of Micomicon—a land of Alnaschar—a place of fairies—a world of dreams—— They were going to it all. Between the walls where no man had ever looked. Death! A magnificent adventure, with Carla in his arms! A roaring filled his ears. They were traveling swiftly now. His

152

senses grew less distinct, like colors merging one into another in a sunset sky. Queer, why it should end like this, after years of life—he—and Carla—together—as it must have been intended from the beginning. A glorious graciousness of Fate, an immortal symphony of fulfilment—to pass on like this with Carla, no matter how many hundred centuries had gone before! And someone—his wife—had said—that seconds meant more than years—when—like this——

The roaring was an enormity of sound. Its wailing was like the wind in the cave of Æolus, its thunder like Stentor's blasts rumbling through the empty bowels of the earth. They numbed and anæsthetized, yet left him with a shred of living, thinking cells which told him they were tearing through the gullet of the gorge, and which, at the same time, held his arms unyielding as bands of steel about Carla's body.

Although close to the edge of an abyss of utter darkness, consciousness did not quite leave him. Vaguely he experienced the thrill of being transported out of a hell of tumultuous sound into a soft and gently drifting sea which was without noise or violence. For an interval he fancied his arms were wings and that he was trying to fly, making rather a bad mess of it because one side of him refused to coördinate with the other. This was the arm, only one arm now, which held Carla. With the other, after a little, he found himself clawing and digging into something. A man may live a hundred years, but when he is ready to die and looks back over the path he has traveled, it seems very short, and the hundred years no more than a few hours. Paul had reflected upon the illusory and baseless fabric of time, its inadequacy and the hollowness of its human measurement. "One who is happy has but a fleeting vision of life," Carla had said to him once. "To live long and terribly, one must be unhappy—in prison." It was odd why he should be thinking of this as he continued to claw and dig. But time

154

had fastened itself upon him like a leech, and if each second of his wide-awake life had been as long as these few seconds he would have lived a thousand years. During this cycle of his existence he slowly and tediously progressed, until, with air filling his lungs again, and the smothering folds of near-insensibility breaking away from him, he knew that he was no longer in water, that his fingers were clutching at soft sand, and that the burden which he had dragged with him was Carla.

There was scarcely a breath between this knowledge and the full and poignant possession of very faculty with which his brain was capable of being inspired. But darkness, mystery, the defeat of death, and the fact of his own physical salvation were submerged all at once in an agonized appeal to the limp, dead form which he clasped in his arms. The spirits of the sable blackness about him listened to his voice calling Carla's name as he struggled to bring life back into her body. Once he had worked over a little girl who had

155

been taken from the water, and now memory came to him vividly of the first gentle beating of the heart again, the slow returning of the soul into the tender body, until the child lived and breathed once more. But Carla's soft breast gave no response. Her lips were cold and lifeless, and, at last, believing her surely dead, he held her face close to him, and kissed her mouth and eyes, as the father of the little girl had kissed his child when she was returning to him. When the first whisper of breath came from Carla's lips he was holding her like this, staring into the blackness. Her heart, beating faintly, responded to the call of life close against his own. Her lips grew warm. Her eyes opened. Paul kissed her again in the blackness that shut them in and found that she was alive.

He did not cry out or speak, but brushed her thick, wet hair back and pressed his face close to hers, and waited. In her first consciousness Carla's arms crept about his neck. Her lips breathed his name. Words were futile for a little while. Only in silence could they claim each other, a silence of voice, where other sound was moaning and throbbing about them. Both knew what it meant as the seconds counted themselves off. They had come through the mouth of the gorge, and were caught in a subterranean hole of the earth. Chance. A miracle. God. That they might have each other at last, with the barrier between them torn away. This was Carla's thought, and her arms drew closer about Paul. He belonged to her now, for there was no other world than this—a pit of gloom with death for its walls, an abysmal grave, where love, for a space, would build for them "the great world's altar stairs that slope through darkness up to God."

She almost spoke the words. Instead she whispered:

"It was right for me to come, Paul? You are—glad?"

"I know—now—that I expected you," said Paul.

Chapter IX

AFTER a time they were standing in the blackness.

More distinctly the hollow, rumbling sound about them began to impinge itself upon their ears as Paul supported Carla against his breast. They listened, as if for a voice, his lips pressing against her hair, where they had so long wanted to rest. What they heard was unlike anything out in the world of sun and sky. The roaring and wailing were gone, and in their place was a phantom-like cadence that moved and stirred about them, but which seemed to come mostly from a vast dome over their heads. It was like something trying to escape, throbbing until it seemed to be beating with little clubs at the drums of their ears when it was nearest, then leaving them to intone and hum like a huge

161

tuning fork through the shut-in sea of gloom. There was no break in the sonorous sameness of it. It was eternity of sound without change. In a little while it could drive a living thing mad.

Paul was fighting against his horror. Where fear had failed to possess him in the drowning grip of the undertows he was now chained by a grimmer thing. It was because of Carla. A few minutes ago the presence of her body in his arms had filled him with an inspiration of happiness in moments of swiftly approaching death; now that they were alive, with air about them to breathe, his heart began to shrink from their fate with an almost malevolent aversion. One should be happy in dying. He had always thought that. The recognition of the beauty of death had become a part of his religion. It was a gift of God, a reward for having lived decently. He had never been afraid to die, but fear was beginning to creep upon him in these moments. Here was a hell, a hopelessness of dungeons, an everlasting scowl of night, with madness for its end. In this Gehenna of torment their minds and bodies were destined slowly to disintegrate in a way that seemed unclean and evil. Swiftly he measured the significance of the strange darkness and stranger sound, while the spirits of Abaddon and Apollyon twisted at his soul. Under rock walls, with a mountain over it, was the stomach of Lucy-Belle's monstrous serpent. Miraculously they had come into it, alive, but no miracle could be great enough to take them out. As if darkness had suddenly given way to light, he saw a picture of their tomb, and the sight of it turned him coward. His arms betrayed him as they closed crushingly and afraid about Carla, holding her from what he saw. In answer, her hand came to his face and pressed it gently. He was amazed that it should be so warm. He was more amazed by the softness and sweetness of her lips when they found his in the darkness.

"I am not afraid," she said. "Are you?"

Her voice was no different than if the sun had been shining, and there was something in it for him which had never been there before. A kind of exultation came with it, a gladness which trembled in the darkness, and which sent shame and triumph sweeping over him in a submerging emotion.

"Afraid? Good God, no!"

She drew herself out of his arms and stood beside him, with her hand in his. Their voices had broken down a tenseness about them, and life drew closer, more sure. He wanted to see her, and fumbled in his sodden pocket for his metal box of matches.

"I'm going to strike a light, Carla. I want to look at you!"

A flare of yellow flame made a hole in the blackness. Until it died out their eyes devoured each other. Carla was like an angel. Love, transforming death into a happy incident, was an uncovered glory in her eyes at last, clearly revealed for him to see.

164

He knew that only the positiveness of their fate could make her look at him like this, with Claire living and waiting in another world outside. Claire seemed infinitely removed from him, a century away, a glow of memory—like star dust, yet he thought of her as the match went out. His wife would go on living. He and Carla were about to die. He had seen understanding and sureness in the shining depths of Carla's eyes when the tiny flame had illumined their faces. She had let him know, without words, that earth bonds were stricken from her, because there was no longer an earth for either of them. For a few hours they were to be in a world all their own. Then—their couch of everlasting sleep—together. He felt a spiritual reaction from the oppression of horror and fear which had come upon him. To feel sure that Carla knew, and that she had given herself to him because of her knowledge—that she was not afraid, but was happy in the freedom which an approaching termination of life made possible for them, filled him with an emotion which took from their brief future its stark and ugly grimness and gave to it an almost joyous aspect.

As if she had been a partner in the few seconds of his thoughts, Carla spoke softly, giving him her hand again in the night which shut them in.

"I want to hear you say it, Paul! I have dreamed, and even prayed in my wickedness, and have fancied your voice telling me the story. For that I have many times asked God to forgive me. But now it is right and just. I want to hear you say—you love me."

"I do," said Paul. "I know—now—that I have loved you from the beginning of time, before I came to the Mistassini, before I was born in this life—a thousand or a million years I have worshiped the soul that is you. Sometime, it may have been ages ago, I know that you belonged to me."

"I have always belonged to you," said Carla. "Yours is the love I thought was hopelessly gone from me—up there. But to die with you is my right. Can there be such a thing as doubt for us now?"

"I am sure there cannot," he said.

"You would like to live?"

"Without you, no."

"And there is no chance—no hope of saving ourselves?"

"I can conceive of none. No force could contend with the maelstroms in the throat of the chasm. At the other end all physical matter is ground to pulp as the water comes out through the gorge. We are caught between the two."

He calmly and frankly spoke the truth to her. She made no reply in words, but he could feel her response creeping through her finger tips to him, could feel the tremble and thrill of it in her body. He had not frightened her, but had dispelled from her the beginning of a fear. She did not want to live. The truth seized upon and helped him with a kind of shock. Yet it was a simple thing, one he

167

should have known without intuition or discovery. For Carla was—not only a woman, but a *soul*. Back there, in Claire's world, she would be lost to him—no matter what he might do in the way other men had solved such problems. Only here, in a beginning and an end all their own, could she belong to him.

Again she was in his heart, listening to his thoughts.

"It is strange, but I want to sing in this darkness," she said. "I did not know that blindness could be so beautiful!"

"Nor I!" he answered.

Chapter **X**

ONE can follow the Big Gorge for a distance after it comes out from its hiding place under what is called a mountain in the edge of the Laurentian country. But, for a mile or so, only a squirrel or some other clawed thing can climb so that it may be looked into. At least men have not tried it. After this it widens, and a hundred feet down are glimpses of frothing furies, which, farther back, send up a faint rumble through the earth. At last the gorge ends, and the water which has run the gauntlet of its walls rushes forth into tranquillity. One might regard it as the dead thing which was once water, so thoroughly has it been pounded and cut to pieces. People say that no physical thing can come through the gorge. This, of course, must be an error, for logs and river driftage cannot be utterly ground to pieces, and in time the gorge would become choked with its own undigested, lifeless matter.

During the night following Paul's accident and Carla's leap, men were active below the gorge. Derwent lost no time in racing back to the Mistassini, and the presence of a hundred men below the chasm before midnight was the result. Every device of engineering science and unlimited resource which might be employed came with them. The big pool at the foot of the gorge was a glare of illumination, and men went down the river with their flaming torches, afoot along its banks and in canoes between them, questing for a shred of something which a few hours before might have been a part of Paul or Carla.

Lucy-Belle, shocked into sickness, was taken to her home. But Claire remained. Men who saw her in the weird glow of the lights will never be able to forget the image of her face as it was photographed upon their

172

memories. Her blue eyes were so wide open
and staring, so filled with an unwavering
sapphire flame that at times Derwent thought
of her as a spirit-goddess instead of a woman.
Could Paul have seen her he would have
known that at last she had conquered her
fear and repugnance of the wilderness. She
had come with the first men before a trail
was cut. Her dress and shoes were torn, her
soft skin bruised and bleeding. Where the
water crashed and thundered loudest out
from between the chasm walls she stood unafraid, until Derwent twice drew her back
from the nearness and danger of it. She re-
sented his appeal to leave the search to others,
and Derwent made it only once. A white
face, watching for its dead—that was what
men would remember. Eyes flamingly blue,
hungrily searching the black stream as it
came from the mountain. A fragile form that
seemed tireless as steel. A woman, and yet
more than woman—an unforgettable spirit,

a vision that was like tragic music, always to be remembered.

She did not give up with the first hours of evening, but continued to watch through the night. She did not move from the foot of the gorge and the pool, as if she were sure that whatever came to her would be found there. Derwent was frequently with her, and tried to talk, but her lips framed few words. Not until day came again did something give way in her, and hopelessness take its place. Then he took her home to Lucy-Belle.

"I waited too long," she said to him, and afterward, back with the searching men, he wondered what she had meant.

These searchers, could they have looked through rock, would have seen a fire. It was the second night for Paul and Carla in a place where night and day were the same. Paul had found drifts of wood along the edge of the sand, mixed with pitchy pine, and a little spot in their world was illumined by light. With blazing torches they had explored its walls and limits until the map of their universe was an indelible picture in their minds —except that part of it which hung in vast and empty blackness over their heads, an infinity whose depths the light they made fell short of measuring. They had plumbed its pitilessness to the core.

In the fire glow sat Carla, combing her long, silky hair with her fingers. Paul watched her as she smoothed and braided the tresses, employing as great care as though she were in her bedroom at home. This was the third time she had given it such attention in their thirty-six hours of entombment. At other times he had held a light for her at the edge of the water while she bathed her face and hands, and once she had said to him: "It is wonderful water, almost as soft as that which comes with rain." She spoke as if they might have been camping on one of the streams they loved, with the sky above and flowers about them. It was her utter acceptance of their fate as a thing of happiness which transformed what would have been a hell for him into a heaven. She had sat in the soft sand at his feet, a few moments before, with her head pillowed against his knees, and there she had unbraided her hair for him to caress, as she watched and pointed out for him the unusual and beautiful pictures that built themselves in the changing coals and crumbling embers of the fire.

Now she was a little distance from him, and no sense of dread or fear oppressed him as he followed the rhythmic movements of her slim white fingers braiding her hair again.

If it were madness which possessed him it was a beautiful madness, a sense of joyous living where there should have been despair. At first the fighting part of him had instinctively struggled against it, but now he accepted it fully, until, seeing Carla as she was, death seemed vague and far away and the glory of life very near. They had made no effort to hide from themselves the coming

176

of the end, and Carla thought of it as a beautiful thing, a little journey, which they were making gladly together. Never had Paul believed so surely in a God. He had found himself fond of telling her how he loved her hair more than any other physical thing about her, and she had said: "I am going to spread it out so you may put your face in it when we lie down to sleep." This was the way she spoke of what was to come—as sleep. To drift off like this, his arms about her, seemed to Paul the fruition of a great privilege and joy, and not a triumph of fleshly dissolution. He had told her little stories about his mother and of the time they had spent sun-filled hours in the Indian burial place at Brantford, where the proudest of her forest ancestors were buried.

"I could not understand her then, when she told me how gladly she would give her life, were it not for me, to live for a single year the glorious freedom of Molly Brant," said Paul. "But I do—now. In that one year

177

she knew she would find something which would more than make up for all the other years she might live, just as every hour here with you is more to me than ten thousand back there."

As he said these things, and believed and felt them, there was in him a will to live which would not utterly extinguish itself. It was scarcely more than a spark, a smoldering ember that was bound to die, for his eyes, his brain, and every faculty of reason which he possessed told him there was no hope of finding a way beyond the walls which shut them in. A few minutes before, when Carla had sat at his knees, with his fingers feeling the warmth and sweetness of her hair, this spark had leaped into flame. It still remained as Carla yielded at last to his demand, and gave herself to the bed he had made for her, with his coat for her pillow.

"It seems almost a sin to sleep," she said; and if slumber were near, or even the necessity for it, he could find no shadow of it in her face. She might have risen from her bed an hour ago, so freshly clear and lovely were her eyes, so deep their lustrous content and happiness when she looked at him. Yet, after a little, her lashes drooped as if to veil the love behind them, and lay in velvet darkness against the whiteness of her cheeks. For a while Paul sat close and watched her, and with each breath the flame in him grew stronger, the demand that something happen, through force of God or man, to break down the walls of death which environed her.

Alone, with Carla's unconscious form lending faith and inspiration to his thought, he fixed his attention, as a dozen times before, on the smoke which rose from the burning wood.

Where did it go?

Hours ago he had asked himself this question, and until he had discovered a thin fog of smoke settling over the water, and drifting away with the rush of it, his blood had run swiftly with a thrill of hope. And now,

179

in spite of the fact that he *knew* where it went, the question remained, as if a voice inside his head had been trained to ask it, parrot-like, and could not be made to stop.

He and Carla had collected a pile of pitch-wood. As they had found each stick they had acclaimed it a treasure discovered, until the thrill of a game had become part of their endeavor. He chose a stick heavily weighted with pitch and lighted the end of it in the fire. Then he walked off into the gloom where he and Carla had gone many times before. It was like following the inside of a great rock drum which was flat on one side —flat where the water thundered and raced through the mountain.

When his torch burned short he returned for another. Carla had not moved in her sleep, and he buried himself in blackness again, following the rock wall so closely that his body touched it, trying at every step to pierce with his vision a little farther into the stygian pit over his head. It was into this pit

180

that the smoke went, mounting in drifting spirals, like smoke in an Indian tepee. Up there, he thought, it was taken by a slowly dragging current of air made by the suction of the stream, and descended to exit from the mountain with it. There was only one break in the circular wall of gruesomely black and water-worn rock, against which, in ages past, a subterranean flood had washed and roared. This was where a small section of it had given way from overhead and had piled up a mass of broken stone which he had climbed, with Carla watching from below. Here the smoke from his torch did not go upward but settled about his head and disappeared toward the vent in the mountain through which the river rushed with great force. He went to this outlet. It was a hole which his eyes were unable to measure, choked to within a foot of its upper jaw by a seething flood of water, and out of which—though the space for sound was small—came such a sullen rumbling that his blood was chilled as he listened to it. Alone, he would have plunged into this. To die fighting, pitting his small strength against all the forces which might oppose him, was the urge which was refusing to subdue itself within him. He flung out his flaming torch and saw it swallowed in an instant. Like that he would have gone if Carla had not been there to go with him.

He turned back to the fire and put on a fresh stick of resinous wood before he sat in the sand near enough to Carla to touch her with his hand. He wondered if fear had begun to seize upon him as he looked at her unconscious form, foreseeing the torment of impending hours when madness would be for him alone. Unless they died together, he must outlive Carla—to save her from a realization of that which he, in his greater strength, should bear. And yet, was he stronger than she? He knew he was afraid when this thought came to him for an answer. For with it rose a vision of Carla beside her dead, a spirit of undying fearlessness and faith, with a prayer in her heart until the end. Even as she slept he saw the sureness of what he visioned in the tranquil beauty of her face. There were shadows on it which exhaustion made, but these were softened by the other thing, until, through the mysterious alchemy of a woman's heart, they gently merged themselves into her loveliness. He held himself from awakening her, yet he wanted her awake. Iron hands drew him to his feet, and a third time he lighted a pitchwood flambeau at the fire.

Chapter XI

PAUL knew he must keep moving, or rouse Carla from her sleep. The nakedness and desolation of aloneness were turning him into a coward. Not a coward who was afraid of death, but one who felt increasing horror in passively waiting for it. He went to the débris of rock again. He had no reason for this, no thought, except that it offered him the one chance to do something physical besides fumbling his way over unstable and shifty sand. The desire for a work to do was an ache in his body as well as his brain, and he began to climb the broken mass, as he had done once before. He had gone about thirty or forty feet above the floor of their dungeon then, but this time he found footholds which carried him a little farther, until, from the point he reached, he could look over the bulge in the rock which had previously concealed their fire, and could clearly see Carla in the glow of it.

He had the desire to call to her, to feel her glorious life a part of their existence again. Sleeping, she seemed gone from him. He swung his torch, making a writing of fire in the blackness, and his lips almost cried her name. Then he recognized the weakness of his act and began to pull himself a little more up the broken wall.

If Carla had awakened and turned her eyes toward him, she would have seen a strange and weird thing. The burning piece of pitchwood was a spout of yellow flame, illumining at times the ghostly figure that bore it, and then floating alone in a limbo of midnight emptiness as if borne by shades that in color and spirit were a part of the gloom. She might have thought, rousing herself from slumber, that hands which were no longer Paul's were bearing it toward the roof of their world. Steadily up into this pit of

Acheron it went, and there it disappeared, as
if smitten by a mighty breath that extinguished it in a second. For a time utter darkness lay where the light had been. Then the
torch reappeared as suddenly as sable wings
had engulfed it, and in another moment it
was plunging down through space. In a few
minutes Paul came where it had fallen sput-
tering in the sand, and picked it up again.
More than ever his face was like that of a
ghost. His cheek was marked by a bleeding
wound. His shirt was in shreds on his breast.
His eyes blazed in a way that would have
startled Carla.

He went to the edge of the water and
bathed his face and hands. Then he returned
to the fire and knelt beside Carla. He raised
her head gently in his arms, and she did not
awaken. He held it against his breast and
kissed her hair.

"Carla!" he whispered.

Her lips moved, her lashes trembled, and
opened slowly to unveil her eyes.

189

She was looking at him in another moment, with her hands at his face. His arms closed more tightly about her, and his voice sounded strange as he told her what had happened.

"You have slept a long time," he said. "At least—it seemed long—and I took a torch and climbed the pile of rocks again. I went higher than before—so high that I came to a ledge, and followed it—and then I came to a great crack in the wall, and there, at the end of it—I saw—*light.*"

"Light!" she breathed.

"Yes, light. From the sun. I have found a way out."

There was silence then. Almost without effort, it seemed to Paul, Carla crept out of his arms. He knew that something was going with her—forever. Her face was whiter than his own. What he had dreaded to see lay in her eyes—a thing fighting back and crushing the glory which had lived in them for a little while. The understanding of what his discovery meant came quickly to her, and he saw a fabric of assembled dreams going to pieces, like one of the odd jumble pictures on a screen. When its hundred disintegrated parts came together again, they formed Claire's face, waiting for him at the end of the trail of light sent to guide them back to an earthly destiny still unfulfilled, and which, for a time, had passed centuries away from them.

Carla rose to her feet and gazed past him into darkness, and so strangely did her eyes dwell on empty space that Paul could only look at her and wait for her to speak.

"A way out," she said, after a little, as though to someone she was seeing beyond their circle of light. "God coming to us like this, taking us back to freedom and—life. And this little world—*ours*—gone!"

Paul knew the thing he wanted to say would come in a moment, the thing he had made up his mind to say to her when he came down from the rocks. It was a fury of emotion, rolling up slowly through his birthright of stoicism into a storm of speech—a passion of desire breaking loose, a bitterness against life as it had been given him to live, a determination to turn it his own way at last.

Before she could move his arms were about her.

"I have lived a hell in this place," he cried. "Not because I was afraid to die, but because in dying I knew I would lose you. Only in life can I have you, and I want life because of that. You say it is God showing us a way out! It is just as true that God gave you to me here. That world up there means nothing to me—except with you in it. It, too, has been a hell for me. Now I'm going to make it a heaven. I won't let man-made law and convention stand in the way of what is right and intended to be. You are mine, and I shall have you and keep you, one way or the other. We'll face the world together, and tell it so—or we'll go out there and never let it

192

know we live. It is for you to say which it shall be!"

Steadily her hands had pressed against him, and with that pressure came such a change in her face that the fierceness of Paul's arms relaxed, and he saw an idol crushed and broken in her eyes. To the level of that ruin he had sunk his own ideal of Carla. He let her move away from him, and stood with a grim, set face before her.

"I'm sorry," he said. "I know you are thinking that I am vile and unclean."

"Not that," she spoke quickly. "I would rather think I am the one who is unclean."

That was all she said, and he made no effort to answer her. Words became futile, even impossible, as she looked at him. What he might have said, his pleading, the arguments he had built for himself, and for her, crumbled under the tragedy which had come like a sickness into her white, beautiful face —a tragedy that was filled with appeal, with pain, and for a moment or two with an utter

193

loneliness, as if she had lost something which
could never come back to her. He had seen
the same look in her eyes the night her
mother died. Then it had filled him with a
great pity. Now its tenderness, its yearning
for a thing gone, shook him to the foundation of his soul. He saw Carla as he had always
known she would be when it came to her
love for a man. Only a love that had no scar
of ugliness upon it would she take to her
breast and hold there. The memory of love,
its burned-out ash, a love that was crippled
and blind but clean, she would cherish with
the sacred faithfulness of an altar nun. But
not such a love as he had offered her—a theft,
though it could be made a legal theft, from
another woman. Even as he felt this crushing
sense of his loss of her, another emotion, a
freeing of his spirit, a rejoicing with his
grief, entered into him. Carla, as she stood
before him, he could worship through all
eternity. The Carla he had asked for, yield-
ing to him, would have descended out of

194

heaven to the level of his own debasement. Clearly as she had seen his passion and felt the crush of his arms, Carla now saw this change in him, and slowly, believing joyously, a miracle wrought itself in her face, and all that Paul had seen broken down built itself up again.

Softness came into her mouth, and she smiled at him.

"Shall we go, Paul?"

He bowed his head, then picked up the coat which had been her pillow and shook the sand from it.

"Yes. The cleft in the rock faces west, and I think the sun was setting when I found it. If we can get out before dark and make a racket, someone may be near enough to hear us."

He lighted a torch, and they walked across the sand together. At the pile of rocks he took her hand, helping and guiding her, until they came to the beginning of the ledge from where he had looked down on her sleep-

ing form beside the fire. He told her about it
as they paused for a moment's rest.

"I could see your hair lying in a shining
rope across your breast," he said. "You made
me think of one of the fairies which Claire
said might live here."

It was a triumph to speak his wife's name
in the sure, calm way in which it came from
his lips.

Carla looked at the fire in the pit of gloom
below them. It was dying out. The yellow
pool of light was narrowing and growing
dimmer.

A sob came in her throat.

"We won't need—ever—to forget," she
said.

"No, never."

"Especially—the little fire."

"And you—sleeping beside it," added
Paul.

They continued upward. The fire was shut
out. The ledge widened and turned, so they
were going through a tunnel in the rock,

196

where water had once made its way to underground depths. They had gone only a short distance when Paul stopped and smothered his torch in the sand until its flame was extinguished. After that they saw a pale reflection of light ahead of them. When they reached it they could look up through a long, narrow fissure that sloped steeply, with day at the top of it. It was a two or three hundred-yard climb, littered with broken rock, which half choked the ascent in places. A mass close to them had freshly fallen.

"I spoiled my shirt in that," said Paul. "I loosened the stuff and came down with it. I hope there isn't another place like it farther up."

Talking about a shirt when they were coming in this way from under the shadow of death sounded stupid and out of place. And the unutterable thing which possessed them, their deadening lack of exultation, seemed even more hopelessly incongruous. A detonation reached them faintly. Engin-

197

eers were using dynamite somewhere down the river in an effort to find their bodies. What an unearthly drama it would be, Paul thought—coming upon their friends as they would soon be doing, like spirits returning from the dead. Yet he was not thrilled. There was light enough for him to see how terribly Carla was fighting for the courage to face their unexpected gift of life. She was trying hard, like himself, to force upon herself the sheer will of gladness, to appear happy at their deliverance. Each was struggling to help the other, quite frankly and unevasively, knowing that it was not life which mattered so greatly now as their fortitude to bear it as they should. He felt as if they were coming out before an audience in a theater, and that it was Carla, infinitely more than himself, who had the burden to carry.

He led the way over the pile they had to climb, helping her where it was roughest. The fissure was twenty feet wide where he had loosened the rock that had started the avalanche, but above this point it narrowed until in places it was scarcely wider than their bodies, though over their heads its slanting walls steadily drew apart as they progressed, letting down the fading light of day. The climb was more difficult than the one they had made by torchlight from the floor of the cavern, and twice in the next hundred feet they were compelled to make their way almost straight up the walls of the crevice, dragging and pulling themselves by means of jagged projections of rock, that they might pass over what were apparently impassable barriers in their path. They were halfway when the fissure split apart, and they stood in a walled pit twenty feet square, from which a narrow rock-filled corridor continued upward like a precipitous exit from a dungeon.

Paul was breathing deeply from his exertions, and Carla was fighting for breath. He could see where the sharp edges of the stones had bruised the hands which she was holding at her breast. Her skirt was torn, and through a rent in her sleeve the whiteness of her arm revealed itself. Her face was streaked with rock dust, and hollows which he had not noticed clearly before were in her cheeks and under her eyes Over them was a broader light of day. He could have flung a stone up to the level of the earth, and beyond that was a sky of vivid blue, still touched by the glow of a declining sun. It was this light, descending in a pool upon them, which made him see another Carla. The mellowing illumination of the pitch pine, the velvety softening of shadows, the pale unreality of first daylight had concealed things from him. Now they were revealed, betraying a change which could no longer keep itself behind the mask of her courage. Something in her had died since they left the pitchwood fire. The ash of it was in her face, the ghost of it in her eyes, and she knew that he saw it and tried to smile at him bravely. He wanted to take her in his arms, and his lips almost cried out the desire. Carla saw that, too, and when the thing of iron in him triumphed over both voice and act, gratitude eased the anguish in her face.

"I'm glad you understand," she said, as if he had spoken, and knew what was in her mind. "I might run away. That would be easier for me. I could hide myself somewhere, and always remember, and always love you. Nothing can kill those things—memories— and love. I would be satisfied to do that. I would be—almost—happy. But I must do the other thing. I must go to Claire. It will be hard to do that."

Her admission of her love for him was made in a quiet and introspective way, as if his physical self had ceased to be a living part of it. It was this, and her reference to Claire, which strengthened his determination not to weaken her faith in him again.

He moved to the edge of piled-up débris and began to investigate it, cautioning her to stand back a little. The rubble loosened under his feet and slid down. There was quite a little rock slip before he had gone far, sending up a cloud of dust between them. Through this, when it had settled, Carla followed him. She heard him calling to her to go back, but in a moment was standing at his side. Almost above them, so steep was the ascent, the fissure narrowed to half a dozen feet in width and was choked with loose rock and sand. Paul looked at it with somberly appraising eyes and instinctively put himself between it and Carla. Another explosion of dynamite sent a scarcely perceptible tremor through the earth. Slight as it was, a tiny stream of sand and pebbles came trickling down from the suspended avalanche. He caught her hand and took her swiftly back to safety.

"A nearer shot would send that thing down on us," he said. "Wait here until I find out more about it."

"What are you going to do?" she asked.

"First, climb the edge of the wall and see what is beyond."

He did this and returned to her in a few minutes.

"Funny how little things put themselves in our way!" He tried to speak lightly. "The fissure is clear as a floor beyond that slug of débris, which is ready to topple. We could be out in five minutes if it were not for that. As it is, I've got to take a chance."

"And—the chance?"

"We must get over the loose stuff. Either that or go back—to the little fire."

"We must go on," she said.

"Yes, we've got to go on. We passed a stick back there five or six feet long. By hugging close to the wall I think I can reach one of the keystones in the slide and loosen it. It won't be difficult, and the whole thing will come down like a house with the foundation pulled out from under it. I'm going to take you back a distance."

"And when the slide comes, where will you be?"

"Against the rock wall, as small as I can make myself."

"You mean," said Carla, with quick understanding in her eyes, "that you are going to take the stick and pry one of the rocks loose, but not from the edge of the wall, for no foothold is there. Your intention is to stand in front, and make an effort to get out of the way when the avalanche starts."

"I am sure I can do it."

"If it comes slowly, yes. But what if it should come the other way? Let us go together, Paul. It may be that we can get over it safely."

"Wait here until I get the stick."

"If we try to climb over it together we will not need the stick."

"But we cannot climb it. I know. I have seen a hundred of those things in the pit. They are like hair-trigger guns, even when they look solid. It is necessary to loosen a rock

204

*Almost without effort, it seemed to Paul, Carla
crept out of his arms . . .*

and then make a run for it. The stick will give me a few feet start."

"But it may be more firmly fixed than you think."

"My stick will prove it. Until then you must remain here."

She accompanied him to the downward exit of the small, room-like prison they had entered, and listened to his footsteps until the sound of them grew faint. Then she ascended to the crest of the rock slip again. A score of feet beyond lay the danger point. Between it and where she stood was the rough depression, out of which Paul would be compelled to race for his life should he loosen the avalanche. There was an overhang of rock, high up, and she did not see how he could escape it. She turned to look back in the direction he had gone. It was like Paul to take the situation in this way, as if it were an unimportant incident rather than a tragic thing.

Light was fading swiftly, and evening

shadows were falling between the deep, close walls of the crevasse. A radiance was in Carla's face, as if a voiceless spirit within her were sending a message to someone in the world above. She could hear Paul's footsteps returning, the iron nails in his boots striking on rock, and her lips moved, yearning to call his name. Then she ran down into the hollow and up its farther edge. After all, it might not be such a sword of Damocles over them. If it were not, then Paul could only scold. If it were——

She began to climb.

Chapter XII

PAUL heard the crash. He was a little beyond the place where he had left Carla, and ran to it, calling her name. When she did not answer he called to her again, and the stick dropped from his hand and rattled like a dry bone at his feet. He leaped through the dust which was settling quickly and heavily, and saw the hollow choked to the brim with the débris of the avalanche. Carla was caught in the last grip of it, near the crest of the rock slip. The upper part of her body was out, and she was alive when Paul reached her. He tried to speak as he tore at the rocks. But his voice was gone. He saw Carla's eyes looking at him with the light fading out of them. She made no sound. Her eyes were closed when he had her in his arms at last. Yet she was not dead—he found himself saying the words over and over as he climbed with her out of the fissure.

It may be that the full story of Carla Haldan and Paul would never have been known had it not been for the happening of this night. It seems reasonable that neither Claire nor Lucy-Belle nor the others would have told the more intimate of its details. A madman told the story. The madman was Paul. He came into the engineers' camp in the middle of the night. They did not know him at first, for brush and limbs and rocks had disfigured him in the darkness. His face was like that of a man who had been beaten with naked fists. His clothes were half gone. His feet were bleeding through the shredded leather of his boots. In his arms he carried a woman; a dead woman, they thought. Not until Derwent unwrapped the coat with which her head and shoulders were protected and saw her face could he clearly realize that the man was Paul.

They took Carla to the Mistassini.

She was carried gently, but quickly, in a litter—with half a dozen men taking turns in bearing her.

Even then, in his exhaustion, Paul insisted on walking at her side until the last nerve in him broke. It was this which robbed him of a day and a night of conscious life.

When he came to himself again, after hours of torturous sleep, Derwent told him that Carla was badly hurt but would live.

Claire, he said, had returned to her people in New York the second day after his supposed death. Lucy-Belle had gone with her. Word had been sent to her that he and Carla were alive, and Lucy-Belle had replied, saying that Claire was very ill. Then had come a telegram from Claire.

Derwent gave it to Paul.

"I am so happy," it said. *"Come to me as quickly as you can. Only God knows how glad I am."*

"It sometimes takes a thing like this to bring out the love in a woman's heart," said

Derwent, remembering Paul's years of loneliness.

"Yes, it does," said Paul, and he saw Carla's
face between him and the words which
Claire had written.

He went to see Carla soon afterward. He
had taken a great deal of pride in the clean,
white hospital he had built for the company,
and now he blessed it. Derwent told him
what it had meant for Carla. They had X-
rayed her and had made the extraordinary
discovery that there was not a broken bone
in her body. But something had happened to
her back, and she was paralyzed from her
waist down. Temporarily, he believed.
Knowing what Paul would have done under
the circumstances, he had sent to Quebec and
Montreal for expert assistance, to consult
with the company staff.

Carla was propped up against a mass of
pillows in her snowy bed when Paul arrived.
Everything was white about her, except the

rich darkness of her hair—the room, the bed, her lacy gown, her face. Like that, with two silky braids streaming over her shoulders, she might have been a child, one who had been a long time sick, with an exquisite, fragile beauty about her. He had not expected to find her so like a lily-petaled flower whose soul a breath might carry away.

He seated himself beside her, and she let her hand creep over the coverlet to him. It was helplessly weak. Her fingers were only a feathery pressure about his.

"Please don't scold me, Paul," she said faintly, trying to smile. "You see, I was right. If the rocks had buried you, I could never have got you out and brought you home. Could I?"

He did not answer, but held her hand so closely that a joyous little melody of content came for a moment in her throat. "I am glad. I was afraid you would be angry with me. Now I know I shall get well quickly!"

It seemed difficult for them to find things

to say. Paul, fighting, with the grimly set lines of an Indian in his face, was holding back what he wanted to tell her. Carla knew. A little more and she would have cried, her own weakness letting down the thing which both were valiantly making an effort to hold between them. He told her about the specialists who were on their way, and that their own staff had no doubt but that she would very soon be on her feet again. He tried to talk without a strain in his voice, yet he could feel the falseness and pretence of his effort when he wanted to take her in his arms and kiss her pale, sweet face.

Carla knew this, too.

At last, when it was time for him to leave her, she said: "When are you going home?"

"I don't know," he replied.

"It must be soon," she urged. "I want it that way. You must start to-day—or to-morrow. Only that will make me well. Claire wants you. Please—read this——"

She gave him a crumpled yellow slip of

216

paper. It was a telegram, crushed, as if she had been holding it a long time before he came. He smoothed it out and read the words which his wife had sent her. The message was almost identical with the one he had received, giving him the impression that Claire, in the stress of her emotion, had been able to find but a single thought for them both.

"*I am so happy,*" it said. "*Send Paul to me as quickly as you can. Only God knows how glad I am.*"

"She has faith in me," said Carla. "She asks *me* to send you to her. What a privilege that is, Paul, for one woman to give another! No matter how hard I try I can never be as wonderful as Claire. The world does not hold many women like her. She loves you. She wants you. When will you go to her?"

"You said—to-morrow."

"Yes, to-morrow."

He rose, and stood looking down at her.

"I will go," he said. "But sometime I will come for you, Carla. Maybe not now, not in

217

this life, but sometime. May I continue to dream that?"

"It is not a dream," she said. "It is faith. I am giving you up for a little while, that is all. Sometime, in another life, these tests which God put upon us will return you to me."

When he looked back at her from the door she was smiling, her eyes filled with tears.

He tried to readjust himself between the time of this last visit with Carla and his departure for home. His effort was an honest one, a struggle to fit himself to certain demands which he accepted as necessary and inevitable. He was sure of himself as he returned to Claire. It was almost an exultant sureness, which left upon him no sign of spiritual or physical torment. He was possessed now by memories which blessed even as they burned. It was as if somewhere in him were a little song, a part of himself, which said: "I have a room whereunto no one enters save I, alone. There sits a memory on a throne. There my life centers." Carla was the memory. He made no effort to turn away from the truth, or harden himself in his contemplation of it. Someone had said that memory was a paradise from which Fate could not drive one. And the room which had built itself in his heart could never be leveled or taken away from him. It was indestructible, like a soul.

Claire, in a way, became the keeper at the door. Because of her he had closed it, and because of her he would never open it except to himself. He could conceive of no one but Claire in this sacred place. A long time ago, when he was a boy, there had been in his room a picture of an angel with snowy wings and golden hair. She seemed to be floating through clouds, and he remembered that his first ideas of heaven came from this angel and that she inspired him to ask questions which his mother sometimes found difficult to answer. The picture had always remained in his mind. It recurred to him in thinking of Claire. It was impossible for him to feel resentment against his fate, or even a desire to change it, in going to her. There were occasional women at whose breasts the world found its spiritual glory. Claire, he knew, was one of them—like the angel in his room. It was he who had been the misfit in their lives, and this defect in himself he was prepared to remedy—if he could.

He read Claire's telegram many times on the way south. He tried to read between its lines. He tried to understand more clearly the change which had come over her. Derwent had told him how she had watched where the water roared out of the chasm. "Whiter than death, as if she would die unless you came out alive," he had said. And Carla: *"She loves you. She wants you."* And now her own words on the yellow paper in his hand, entreating him to come to her as quickly as he could. There was a strange singing in his heart and a dull grief. If she should love him—at last—like that. After years of waiting, and hoping, and of yearning for a woman to be a part of him—children—a home he had dreamed of——

He folded the telegram for a last time and put it in his pocket.

He was seeing the tears in Carla's eyes.

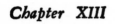

Chapter XIII

PAUL had told only Claire that he was on his way to her. At the station a familiar face came out of the hurrying streams of humanity to greet him. It was Jimmy Ennerdale, whose presence always gave him greater comfort than that of any other man. He had known Ennerdale for a long time, and Claire had grown up with him like a sister. Jimmy had always seemed older than Paul, with a premature grayness in his hair and a slight stoop in his thin, sensitive body. His affection for Paul possessed the unchangeable quality of the marble out of which he was slowly and persistently chiseling fame for himself as a sculptor. He had been working in the West, and Paul had not seen him for a year. Ennerdale had grown older in that time, he thought. His face was thinner, his hair whiter

225

over his temples, his physical tone even less robust than when he had seen him last. He had the same quick, nervous alertness about him, and it did Paul good to see the gladness in his face as they gripped hands. He knew that Claire, unable to meet him herself, had sent Jimmy in her place.

"She is like a child, waiting for you," said Ennerdale, as they rode toward his home. "I was there with Mother last evening, and she asked me to meet you. She cried and laughed and is damnably happy. If you don't mind, I'd like to come over when you two have settled down, and have you tell me about this monstrous happening. May I?"

"You know you don't need an invitation," said Paul. "Come to-morrow."

He had an odd feeling of not knowing what was going to happen as he left Ennerdale and entered his home. He could feel himself under a strain roused by the nearness of explanations which it was Claire's right to hear and his duty to make. It would be hard to talk about Carla, as he must, even should Claire in her wisdom ask for nothing.

Claire was waiting for him in her room. This act of thoughtfulness pleased him. She knew that in a peculiarly embarrassing moment they should be alone. Both were sensitive, each a little fearful of what one or the other might betray in their first greeting. He was thinking this when he went to her. As her door closed behind him, his first impression was of a room filled with flowers. Claire, like Carla, loved them. The air was delicately fragrant with their perfume. Claire was bending over a mass of white roses when he entered, and from these she looked up quickly, and then came toward him with both hands held out. She did not put her arms about him or offer him her lips, yet never had he seen such a light of happiness shining in her eyes. He made a movement to kiss her, but she drew back in such a way that her act seemed scarcely to be repelling him.

"Not now, Paul. Not until we have talked. Then, if you want to kiss me, you may."

She was astonishingly free of the tension which he had anticipated, and as she stood with her fingers clasped warmly about his, telling him how glad she was that he was alive, and how doomed to despair and unhappiness she would have been if he had not lived to return to her, he wondered if it were Claire, his wife, who was talking to him, or another Claire—someone he had never known. For she seemed, all at once, to have drawn herself farther away from him than she had ever been, but in such a sweet and friendly way that the change in her seemed one which could not bring hurt with it.

It was Claire's fight that was hardest. It was going to take a Joan of Arc courage to say what she had planned to say.

She made him sit near her, so they were facing each other.

"Paul, we are going to be honest. You will promise me that?"

228

He knew he was preparing to equivocate as he gave his word. A lie to save Claire from hurt was more creditable than truth. The impulse to shield her, to keep from her all suspicion of his love for Carla, swept over him as he looked at her. She was like the flowers on the table, as easily crushed, he thought. More vividly than ever he saw the difference between her and Carla. Carla would fight on through tragedy, even to death. Claire, suffering more, would droop and fade like a petal in a rose, shrinking from the quicker and more physical action which the other would find for himself. He was not analyzing himself, or her. The thought—like a picture—impressed itself upon him, and Claire, gazing at him in these epic, introspective moments, as if partly seeing the swift visioning in his mind, surprised him by saying:

"Paul, I wonder if you know just how much I honor and respect you. I wonder if you realize how fine you are. I have failed to play my part—as your wife. I have not let you know these things as I should. The fault in our lives is not yours. It is mine. I think I could have made you love me. Yet I saw the unfairness of it unless I could make myself love you first. I hoped and prayed for that."

Darkness coming at midday could not have been more unexpected than what she had said. Acclaiming his integrity, his honor, after what had happened. And in the same breath confessing that she had struggled, even prayed, that she might love him. And with what success?

She was about to tell him. She had drawn a curtain and could not close it until he had seen what lay behind it. Claire, and not himself, was on the witness stand. The fact seemed vague and unbelievable, yet was pressing on him. It was scarcely an intelligible part of his thought when Claire spoke again.

"There wasn't love when we were married, on either side. You did not love me, not in the way you wanted to love a woman, and my feeling for you was an immeasurable respect and admiration for an honorable gentleman. It seems trite and superficial to say that the interests of our families brought us together, does it not? But it is true. I wanted to love you. But I discovered—after a little while—that something was in my way."

"I know," he found himself saying. "You couldn't love an animal, Claire. I was that, until the day you came to the Mistassini. Always the woods, the rough side of life, the things you could not like. It was your Nordic and my Indian—conflicting poles repelling each other. I am going to submerge this part of me. I have been blind and brutal. God knows I am only half worthy of you!"

"And Carla?"

So softly did his wife speak Carla's name that for a moment it seemed as if he had not heard it.

"We have promised ourselves to be honest," she continued. "Do you remember a

231

letter I wrote you from Paris in which I said I was coming to you and that I was sure a more important thing would happen for us in your woods than any journey, like your promised one around the world, could give?"

"Yes, I remember."

"Do you know—now—why I told you that?"

"I have only wondered."

"It was because I had seen, because I had read between the lines of your letters, because I knew at last a great love had come into your life, and that Carla Haldan had brought it to you. You do not love me. You love Carla. And, loving her, you would sacrifice everything for my sake."

His fabric of lies was gone, his soul laid bare under the gaze of his wife's eyes.

"I want to hear you say it, Paul." She was repeating Carla's words whispered to him in the blackness of the earth. "That is why I came to you there. A woman may hide her love from a man, but not from another

232

woman, and it was impossible for Carla to keep her secret from me. Yours was still more open, though I saw you making a magnificent fight. I know, Paul. But I want to hear it from your lips. I must hear it. Do you love Carla Haldan?"

"One word, and the world crashes about us," he said. "Another, and it goes on living. Must you insist, Claire?"

"I must hear you say it. You love— Carla?"

"Yes, I love her."

"More than any other woman in the world?"

"I could only love one woman in that way."

He was conscious of having struck a deadly blow, a hurt he would rather have died than inflict upon Claire. It had dragged itself from him in spite of his determination, and he waited for his punishment, its effect on her. Claire's eyes did not waver. She did not flinch. A starry, radiant light came into

233

her face, and she gave a breathless, half-articulate cry, not of shock or of pain, but of joy. He saw the blood flushing her cheeks, the tenseness leaving her body, and they sat for a time in silence, neither making an effort to speak.

Then he said:

"I thought I would hurt you. And you are glad!"

"Yes, I am glad. I thank God you love Carla."

She rose to her feet, and took a letter from the table. She was trying to keep from crying as she gave it to him.

"I want you to read it and then come back to me," she said. "This evening, if you will, Paul. I lack the courage to tell you things. You will understand when you open it, alone."

It did not seem to him that he was going from his own home when he left her. Nothing seemed the same. Even the roar of the city was a subdued and distant turmoil, like

234

an echo of the eternal moaning he had heard in the bowels of the earth. He went to the Kirke-Durand building and lost himself in the human stream going up with the elevators. On one of the floors was an office, always ready for him. He shut himself in and locked the door.

He opened the letter. There were many pages, closely written in Claire's hand. With almost childish candor they began to tell him of a woman's fight to triumph over herself. There was nothing of vanity or self-conceit about them, and neither were timidity nor humility in what she had put down for him. Like an indestructible redolence they breathed the sureness of Claire's faith in herself. Without emotional effort she told him that unless Carla had come into his life she would never have let him know what she was about to reveal. There was no man in the world more worthy of a woman's love than he, she said. Yet, from the beginning, she had been unable to build her respect and ad-

235

miration into the greater thing she should
have given him. That was one reason why,
repelling the thought of making him care
greatly for her when she could not love him,
she had kept herself away from him so much.
There was another reason, but this was not
disclosed until he had read many pages, each
of which let him look a little deeper into
her heart, and impressed on him a little more
the pride she felt in having been his wife. But
pride was not, and never could be, love. One's
passion for another, in its holiest form, was
guided by a single force. One might stem that
and hold it back, but it was impossible to
make it die. Such a love was Carla's for him.
Then she spoke of another man. It was of
Jimmy Ennerdale, the sculptor, who was
driving his way so persistently to success. She
had accepted Jimmy almost as a brother during her girlhood, but very soon after her
marriage the truth had come to her, she said,
and had grown stronger with each year. She
cared for Ennerdale just as Carla cared for

236

him. It was Paul who might have been her brother, with such frank and unembarrassed simplicity did she confide in him. She knew that Ennerdale loved her, and repeated that a man could not conceal that fact from a woman, though he did not express it in words, and she was sure Jimmy had no idea of her sentiment toward him. This love for Jimmy was the other reason, the more vital of the two, which had held her aloof from Paul. It was not, she thought, a situation in which either should feel the necessity of apologizing to the other. They were taking a twist out of their lives, that was all. She loved Jimmy's work and wanted to become a part of it. She had never held it to be possible, and had not thought of it in that way until she knew that he loved Carla.

Paul finished, and it seemed as though tiny raindrops were falling in his brain, so clearly could he hear and feel the beating of his pulse. In a few moments the moaning of life came to him in a distant wave. It struck nearer in the slamming of an elevator door. Indistinct voices passed down the hall. From another street, blocks away, the hammering of rivet drivers on new steel rose above the rush and roar of traffic. Paul looked from his window, as if he might see the pit, out of which the same sound had come night and day for three years. His eyes fell upon gloomy, sooty walls. Under him lay an unending fabric of men's toil, a great sea of roofs strung with wires, craggy with ugly architectural warts, broken with chimneys, streaked with tarred gutters, and with the gaping, shifting mouths of ventilating funnels sucking air into their artificial lungs. He looked down and saw a thousand moving things, in a stream, like ants, every hurrying particle a human soul struggling in the furious Twentieth Century effort to make itself greater than God. From all this Claire had freed him. She had given him new life, and with it love and happiness. He crushed her letter in his hand as if some pitiful breath

238

might wrench its precious pages from him.

Then he turned to the telephone. It was impossible for him to wait. He wanted to tell her there was one other woman in the world as wonderful as Carla.

In Claire's voice was a trembling note of happiness when he said this.

"Dear old Paul," she cried softly. "But you mustn't come to me until evening. I have something which I must do before I see you again."

That night, when he went to his home, Claire was not there.

She had left a note for him.

"I have gone to see Carla," it said. "Only a woman can make another woman—like Carla—understand."

Chapter XIV

AND here we find ourselves where we began, with the lovely Crippled Lady on her porch at Peribonka.

She had lived a year in Peribonka when we set out to tell this story. A winter had passed, another spring, a summer, and now it was the beginning of glorious September. September is the most beautiful of all months in the Lac St. Jean country. A softness is in the air which one does not feel at any other time, a breath of ripened forests, a soothing warmth and comradeship of earth and water which is like a song. The big river across the road and down the green bank from the Crippled Lady's gardens of flowers is friendliest then. Its water is a sheen of laughter. Its snowy sandbars possess the quality of softened whiteness which gives to them almost

243

the purity of a woman's breasts. It seems crying out for the companionship of men and women and children and all other living things. Birds coming down in thousands from the farther North pause in their flights to remain with it until the first of the black frosts. Bears, fat with their summer's feast of blueberries, like to dig and sun themselves along its shores. Sound carries far in these Indian summer days of the North, and the rippling of its water is like the tinkling of silvery bells—tiny monastery bells, the lovely Crippled Lady says to the children who come to see her, and to whom she tells so many beautiful stories.

There have been changes since she was borne from the hospital to the place, near her mother, where she wants to live. The pit is no longer a pit, but a mighty force driving its energy in unending streams through high-tension wires. The Mistassini may rumble and roar and growl, but it is a slave, securely

244

shackled, and will probably go on laboring for its human masters for all time. This change—or development—was expected, anticipated by experts almost to the day and hour. But others were not. The world, for instance, accepting a very small corner of it as the whole, could not understand why a man like Paul Kirke should deliberately sever himself from the huge prestige and wealth built by his father's success, and, as the story went, bear away with him all his personal possessions in a trunk and a handbag. It could understand, quite easily, how a husband and wife might end their marital relationship, but it was puzzled and shocked that a woman like Claire Kirke should throw herself away, soon afterward, on a stoop-shouldered, prematurely ageing man who was possessed of nothing on earth but an admirable passion for shaping things out of marble.

"There are a lot of people who, taken col-

lectively, are like a big gaping boor," Claire said in a letter to Carla. *"They are amusing for a time. Then they become normal again."*

This was just before she went West to join Jimmy Ennerdale in his work of completing a marble group for an important civic center.

After she got there she wrote Carla:

"It is magnificent. When it is finished we are going to spend a year in Capri, working together."

Capri, the Mediterranean—the habitant country, Lac St. Jean——

"It is glorious here," Carla wrote back. *"I love September!"*

She always sits on her porch so that she is looking up the river toward the north. Paul is there, working out a part of the dream which absorbs them both. Thirty miles beyond the green and blue-black edge of wilderness which she can see Paul has a timber concession, and fifteen men working with him, where a little while before he might

246

have had fifteen thousand. But these fifteen men, and what they are planning to do with the concession, mean more to Paul and Carla than all the millions in the world.

"It is not necessary to slaughter Nature, or even harm her, in order to possess for ourselves some of her products," Paul says in a paper he is writing for a pulp-wood journal. *"There is such a thing as harvesting timber and having a better forest each year instead of a diminished one. Nature wants to fraternize with us, and will, when we cease to sack and plunder her like vandals."*

Next year the fifteen men will be increased to fifty, but now camps are being built and just enough timber harvested to cover the expense of the work. Paul labors with his ax, along with the others, from morning until night.

Every Friday he comes down the river to Carla.

And every day he sends her messages.

This is what happens. As the Peribonka

descends between its sandbars it turns at the head of an island not far from the village, and in a gently sweeping curve forms a big pocket near Carla's home, which has a habit of gathering and holding quantities of driftage which comes down with the stream. This driftage, in the form of wood, the village boys gather for their homes, and now, whenever they find a freshly peeled stick or log, they look for the notches in it, which proclaim it a message from Paul. It is an exciting game, as thrilling for Carla as for the children. The river seems to enjoy it, too, for in one month it brought to Carla five of the hundred or so "messages" which Paul had given into its care, a conclusive proof of its unusual friendship and coöperation. At least, Carla and Paul think so.

Friday is the day Carla is loveliest. Alena, the Swedish woman who cares for the house, is very busy on this day, and both she and the mistress she worships are excitedly preparing and waiting from the time the sun is up.

Carla pays more than usual attention to her appearance this morning, and especially to her beautiful hair, which Paul never grows tired of saying is his most precious possession. She knows about when his gasoline launch will appear at the head of the mile of straight water above the village, late in the afternoon, but she is on her porch, watching the river, hours before that. When the launch comes in sight she remains until she is sure Paul has seen her, and then has Alena wheel her into the cottage. There she waits for him. He has such a furious way of catching her up in his arms, as if she were a little girl, and holding her there, smothered with kisses, that it is the only possible place.

Carla knows that she is going to get strong and well. This mental attitude, her sureness and optimism, together with her great happiness, has overcome the doubt of physicians. She is beginning to stand a little, with Paul's arms about her, and their two precious days a week together are filled with wonderful plans of what she is going to do in another year. Wherever Paul is, there she will also be. That is the point from which they always start in building their castles.

No shadow is cast over their happiness because Carla cannot walk. Paul wheels her about the village in the big chair, and not a cottage is missed in their visits. They go as far as the little picturesque old cheese factory and down the hill to the still older wharf where the boat comes in from across the lake. Dr. Derwent, who is at Mistassini, has allowed Carla to go twice to the monastery, in Paul's launch, and if October is fine she will make her first trip to his concession during that month. Paul takes her over the soft, sandy roads to the edge of the blueberry plains in a buggy, and then carries her in his arms to a place where she can help him pick fruit for their Sunday dinner. He will never give up carrying her like that, he says, even when she is strong again.

Peribonka has grown happier with them.

250

Even Maria Chapdelaine is younger, and Samuel has forgotten his financial losses.

So Carla wrote to Claire:

"It is glorious here. I love September."

Lightning Source UK Ltd.
Milton Keynes UK
UKHW042206070721
386789UK00001B/183

9 781410 107589